To submit a manuscript for our review,

email us at

<u>submissions@majorkeypublishing.com</u>

5

Author's note

Janiece's walk of life takes her on a journey of love, loss, and redemption. This book mentions rape, kidnapping, death, street life, sex, humor, and God. If this book is not for you, then pass over it, but tell someone else about it though. Thank you!

Dedication

To Jaime, my Lil' sis for being there when I needed her to critique my blurb, synopsis and to give constructive criticism when I didn't want to hear it, lol and to put my thinking cap on straight. To my friend Shakima K., a dear friend and to my brother from another mother, Brian D. whom I met in LaGrange.

Love y'all a lot!!!!!!

To the young and old who believe there isn't a way, but there is, and it is through Jesus Christ.

Synopsis

Janiece is a seventeen-year-old who's learned her mama has died from a drug overdose. She spazzes out in anger and holds resentment toward her grandma. She's suffered from verbal abuse long enough. Not dealing with it anymore, she snaps and decides to run away from home and stay with a friend of hers. But freedom ain't all it's cracked up to be. Everything cost in this world. Janiece gets pulled into a whirlwind of parties, drinking, and street life. As she gets on the straight and narrow path, she returns home to her grandparents. She makes some life-changing decisions to better herself through the years. She ends up pregnant and soon her life spirals out of control again. On a dark and lonely night, while standing over a bridge, she thinks about committing the ultimate sin because she's filled with overwhelming emotions.

Never know when you could be entertaining angels...

Josiah, a medical student, has a knack for helping people, but unfortunately while working in the hospital, a patient dies. As he takes a stroll on his break, he sees a woman and decides to rescue her. Little does he know that he's bargain for more than he asks for.

There comes a time for healing…

To be able to heal from her tribulations, she has to do some soul searching. Realizing God has always been in her corner, a minor setback causes her to think Josiah will turn on her like the others. Will Janiece allow forgiveness in her heart and be able to see Josiah as a steppingstone or will she succumb to living in guilt and push Josiah's friendship away?

This book, Trials & Tribulations is about love, loss, and redemption. It may cause painful flashbacks. It might make you cry but it will make you laugh as well.

The Beginning

Chapter 1

2010

Children obey your parents in the Lord: for this is right. Ephesians 6:1.

Janiece

"What happened?" she asked hollering at the top of her lungs.

"Janiece," her grandpa's voice shook with pain.

Frozen in place, Janiece stared at her grandparents and toward the outside, watching the cop reverse out of the driveway.

"Come here, we have to tell you—" her grandpa couldn't finish his sentence as he dropped his head.

"What happened? What's gon' on!" she screamed frantically, closing the front door behind her.

Her grandpa lifted his head slightly and whispered, "Sit down, we have something to tell—" her grandpa flopped down on the sofa and covered his face with his hands.

Janiece knew whatever it was; it was heartbreaking to

hear. She turned her head toward her grandma. Her grandma suddenly dropped her head too.

"Please tell me what's gon' on."

"Your ma…your mama…" her grandma stuttered.

"What? Talk to me," asked Janiece, yelling at her grandma.

"Your mama's dead."

Her world stopped. Her eyes got big. Her thoughts ceased at the moment. She rolled her eyes into the back of her head. Felt a pressure settled upon her chest like a ton of bricks. The hope of recovery was no longer an option. Her mama was dead. She felt the tears release before she shrieked. Her voice shook with sadness. "When? How did she die?"

"She was found in a dope house on Third Street. They say she OD'd," her grandma's voice was low and softly spoken.

Janiece glared at her grandma and shook her head repeatedly. She put her hands over her ears and screamed, "She didn't love me enough. She didn't love me enough!" her thoughts instantly went to the conversation she had with her mama. 'Don't end up like me. I ain't got nothing to show for it. I want you to graduate 'cause you a pretty and smart girl. When you graduate then we can start living together again after I get cleaned. Hearing those words out of her mama's mouth, she felt overjoyed and hugged her mama but that was six years ago.

While in her thoughts, she felt an arm pull her into their body as they walked. She lifted her eyes a split second and recognize it was her grandpa. He was wearing his favorite cologne; Aramis. She bent her head under his arm and cried long and hard. I love you, mama. I miss you, mama. I don't know how I'm gon' to make it in this world without you again. How could you leave me? How could you love those drugs more than me?

Somehow, someway she was in her room. As she lay under the covers, the tears poured. Staring up at the ceiling and feeling drain from life, she closed her eyes wanting to erase the bad memory. To erase the hole in her heart. The emptiness. The heavy feeling in her chest was still there. At a standstill. Maybe it was gas or maybe her heart stopped but she laid in bed, trapped in a false

reality. In a zone. Sleep didn't come until hours later as
she lay there, numb.

The day after

Janiece didn't come out of the room unless it was
imperative. She avoided her grandparents because she
didn't feel like answering crazy questions like how was
she feeling? Where to go from here? How does it make
you feel? Instead of the possibility of the agonizing
interrogation, she felt the need to have a moment with
herself. She picked up the cordless phone and called Mya
who she met through a mutual friend at school. Mya told
her she would get her in an hour.

To her, she looked up to Mya ever since meeting her
in the earlier part of May. Their friendship grew close in a
span of weeks. Like sisters. She was a dear friend that she
confided in. Although their different personality
mismatched, they clicked. Mya was loudmouthed, ghetto,
ambitious, and a nurturer whereas she was quiet,
sheltered, and a follower. She felt loved and secure with
Mya. In Janiece's eyes, Mya had it going on for a
nineteen-year-old young woman with her own apartment,

a boyfriend, a job, and a car.

Janiece dressed in dark jeans, a red top, and some black Nike's. She slipped out of the house without letting her grandparents know. She stood on the corner of Ashton and Alford Street to meet Mya. In the car with Mya, she said nothing. No sound. No movement. She just stared ahead as a song from Lil' Boosie blared from the car speakers.

"What's wrong with you?" asked Mya. "Janiece, why you ain't talkin'?"

Without looking at her, Janiece broke down and started crying.

Mya clutched the steering wheel and turned the volume down. "What's wrong wit chu?" she asked, her voice calm.

"My mom died yesterday," she muttered, her voice barely above a whisper. She recalled the time her mama had lost her job at Piggly Wiggly. Her mama got caught smoking weed in the bathroom by her boss. After being without a job for two years, her mama suffered from mood swings such as low energy, anxiety and being in a depressive state. Oftentimes it bothered Janiece but she was eleven years old. She tried what any normal child would do and that was to love her mama. It didn't help because her mama started disappearing days at a time. Men after men came in and out of their apartment until they left on their own. It was a dark night when she opened the bedroom door and caught her mama snorting white stuff off the nightstand. Her mama looked at her with murky eyes and told her to spend the night with her grandparents. She remembered packing some clothes in a bag and being dropped off by her mama. When Sunday came around, Janiece waited for her mama to come get her but she never did. Her grandparents took her home Sunday evening but an eerie feeling washed over her. She remembered walking into her mama's bedroom to find a letter. It said, "I will always love you but my man needs me more." She knew her mama was gone. It hurt her eleven-year-old heart when she walked out with her grandparents.

"Oh, sorry to hear." Mya placed her hand on her shoulder. "You want to talk about it?"

"Nah, it won't solve anything. My life ain't never gonna be the same again" was all Janiece said. Although her mama abandoned her six years ago, she had hope. One day when she graduated from high school, she and her mama would live together again as her mama promised. During the absent years of her life, she prayed that her mama was getting herself together but her mama lied. Janiece felt like she was alone in this world at seventeen. Just the thought of never hearing her mama's voice or ever seeing her mama again crushed her spirit.

After she chilled with Mya at the mall, she knew it was later than usual when Mya dropped her off at home. She opened the side door to the carport and was hit with her grandma's high pitched voice.

"'Neece, you know you cannot and will not come to my house any time you feel like it. You have a set curfew and it ain't about to change until you become an adult and then you can come and go as you please," her grandma stated in a concerned but sharp tone.

Janiece darted her gaze to the time on the microwave. It was twelve in the morning but she could care less at this point. Her feet felt heavy as she shuffled them along the tiled floor.

"I'm talkin' to you," her grandma shouted. "I understand you needed some time to yo' self but you shoulda called home. You got us worried not knowin' what's goin' in your head," her grandma sighed. "Yes, that was my child but she led her own life. I couldn't do no more. I tried," her grandma's voice seemed sad but it didn't match her body language.

With her head down, Janiece said, "I'm droppin' out of school."

"You what?" questioned her grandma.

"I said," she snapped.

"I heard what you said," her grandma faced the bedroom and shouted her grandpa's name. "Willie. Willie."

Janiece watched her grandpa stroll out the room to stand beside her grandma.

"Tell him what you just told me," her grandma said, putting her hands on her curvy hips as her skin tone darkened to a deep shade of mahogany.

"Baby girl, what is it."

"I'm droppin' out of school," she dropped her head.

"Janiece, I know you're angry but you have one more year left. Your mama wanted you to finish schooling."

Just the mention of her mama angered her. How could she? This void. This stabbing pain in her heart cut deep. There was no healing. Even her grandpa couldn't help her. She twisted her head from him because his words were unwanted. How could he heal the hole in her heart? She was dying on the inside. She suffered in silence and anger. How could she forgive her mama? Can you leave me alone, dang! Janiece was troubled in the spirit because she resented her grandma at the moment.

All the times her grandma belittled her came rushing back. She couldn't watch music videos on BET or MTV because it showed living a 'fast life'. She couldn't stay out all night. She had a curfew. She couldn't spend the night with any of her friends. She couldn't sleep in bed past eleven a.m. on the weekends. "Get up 'Neece, it's eleven o'clock. Laziness brings on deep sleep. You're gonna end up like yo' mama cause she used to lay down all day long. And look what that got her." She couldn't wear certain clothes because they brought attention to fast tail boys. She just couldn't and small things like that irritated her over the years. She knew whose daughter she was but she wasn't her mama. Having a child and leaving her with the grandparents because sex, drugs and men were about that life. Little did she know that her grandma's degrading ways were teaching her how not to love? And now she was acting as she cared. It baffled her. She lifted her head and stared at them. She couldn't hold them in any longer. A pool of tears came cascading down her cheeks.

"I knew this day would come, but I didn't know how bad it would affect you. I shoulda did more. It's my fault!" her grandma exclaimed, placing her hands on her heart.

Her grandpa's gentle tone announced, "'Neece, don't beat yourself up. We were hopin' your mama was gonna straighten up. Don't blame yourself for that."

Janiece yelled, "I can't take it anymore!"

Her grandparents looked at each other then back at

her.

"I get it. Grandma, you don't love me. You never did," she stated huffing and puffing, shooting daggers at her grandma.

"What're you talkin' 'bout?" her grandma asked in an offended tone.

Janiece recalled on her hand how many times her grandma disrespected, belittled, and trashed talk about her and her mama. "I've always respected you. Trying to do right and be the dutiful grandchild but you've told me that you were too old to be raisin' kids. I'm gonna end up just like my mama. That's not love. And I can't take it. I'm done!" she yelled, excusing herself from the living room.

"I love you," her grandma cried.

Janiece stopped abruptly. She could hear her grandma's words ricochet in her head. 'You can't seem to do anything right without me yellin' at you. Just lazy like yo' mama. 'You're gonna end up pregnant like yo' mama. Anger shot through Janiece's eyes as she stared at her grandma. Glancing over her shoulder and muttered,

"You don't love me!"

Her grandpa marched to her. "Janiece, don't talk to your grandma like that. We didn't raise you like that. I understand you're upset. We're not gon' talk about this anymore tonight. I know you're out of school and we're gon' to take time this summer to get through with this but I hope you get this stayin' out late and disrespectful talkin' out of your system. We're gon' to bed and we'll find a way to settle this in the mornin'," her grandpa said as he kissed her on the forehead. He encircled his arms around her and held her. "Everything will work itself out in the morning. I'm gon' go say a prayer and 'Neece, I love you, baby girl," he stated as he released her and grasped his wife's hands and led her to their bedroom.

Her eyes followed them as they entered their room before she shut the door to her own bedroom. She sat on the edge of the bed and rocked. She had to come up with a solution. She reached under the computer desk and pulled out a sheet of paper. She grabbed a pen from her book bag. Her right hand wobbled as she wrote to her grandparents a letter. Maybe she was like her mama in one aspect of her life because when the road got rough the going was tough and she wanted the freedom to live her best life so she bounced. There the note lay upon her desk unhidden knowing they would find it.

Grandpa, I know you wanted me to finish school but I can't continue to stay with grandma tearing me down. Day in and day out. You've always said that I had my whole life ahead of me but I don't see it that way anymore. I'm torn because of my mama but I do appreciate y'all takin' me in those years ago. Maybe this time apart will show me what real love is. I love you and I'm sorry to disappoint. But I need to find me and that is to live life on my own and away from y'all.

She opened her bedroom door and retrieved the cordless phone from the kitchen. She dialed Mya's number. She gathered a duffle bag and a book bag of clothes and set the alarm for one in the morning because her grandparents got up before the crows croaked. She wanted to be gone way before they could talk some sense into her.

Chapter 2

Poverty and shame will come to those who disdain correction...Proverbs 13: 18.

Janiece

Beep. Beep.

The alarm startled Janiece as she jumped from her sleep, reaching over to silence the ringing. She dialed Mya's number again. The phone rang three times.

"Mya, Mya—" She heard other people's voices and none sounding like her friend. "Mya!" she whispered. The tunes from a Ying Yang song played in the background. She reared her head back and her gaze focused on the call. If Mya don't come to this phone, I know something. Suddenly, she heard Mya's voice.

"Hey girl, you ready for me to get you?"

"Yeah, how far are you? What're you doin'?"

"I'm leavin' a friend's house and I'll be there in twenty minutes," was all Mya said before disconnecting the call.

Janice kept glancing out the window to spot Mya's

car. Suddenly a car with low beams pulled into her grandparents' driveway. The car idled and flashed the low beams two times. She gathered her bags, tiptoed through the house, and slid out of the door toward the carport. She twisted the knob and released it when the door was shut. I'm finally free! She thought as she hopped into the car.

"Dang girl, I can't believe you actually left home. I thought you were playin' all the times you said you wanted to leave. But I see you're for real this time." She eyed her bags in the backseat of her car. "You think they gonna look for you?" Mya asked while driving.

Janiece didn't answer. She stared straight ahead. She was there physically but mentally she was out of her mind.

"Nah, I don't think my grandma will miss me," she stated while thinking of her former life. Nothing could amount to the feeling of losing a mama. Whether she was around like a real mama or not, losing a mama hurt. It meant all hope was lost. She snorted a cynical laugh when she recalled the day her mama left her for cocaine.

That hurt like hell.

"Where you gonna stay?" Mya asked.

Janiece looked up. "I was hopin' that I could crash with you for a while. I don't have nowhere to go."

Mya cut her eyes at her friend. This bitch is dumb as hell. "You think you shoulda stayed home then? I mean I ain't gonna be watchin' over you like no baby. You stay with me then you got to work or something."

"I can work."

"What about school?" asked Mya.

"I'm droppin' out. Ain't no need to go. My mama didn't go when she didn't want to."

"Yeah, that was yo mama. I got my high school diploma. You know there's a better chance to get a job if you have your high school diploma. Better than that is a degree, but I ain't gon' that far in life."

Janiece didn't comment. She sat staring ahead.

"How soon you gonna look for work? I ain't never brought no otha female in my apartment to stay. I mean I got a man that stay at my crib er' now and then. I don't know what he's gon' say."

"I'm gonna look real soon," she paused in thought. "You don't care where he's at when he's not stayin' with you?"

If looks could kill, Janiece supposed she'd be dead by the look Mya gave her. "Nah. What he do is what he do. I ain't sayin' nothing unless something goes down," Mya responded in a nonchalant tone. Mya recalled the day she graduated from high school, she met Derrell through a mutual friend of hers and moved in with him. She was eighteen. He was twenty-five years old. In the beginning, he laced her with money in an exchange for small favors. And then shopping until she was caught up into the game.

To steer the conversation elsewhere, Janiece asked, "Where do you work?"

"I work at Goody's, the one in the mall. After I work, I party. So if you're gonna be stayin' with me, then its gon' feel like the party never stops. You might hate it or you might love it. All I'm sayin' is you're not a child but an adult. What you do is what you do and what I do is my business."

Soon they were pulling up to Mya's apartment complex. The apartment yards were separated by tiny sidewalks that led up to the front entrance. She grabbed her bags and followed Mya. Her friend didn't offer to help with her bags so she struggled as she carried them to the second floor. Breathing hard, Janiece had to catch her breath.

"Why you breathing so hard on my neck?" Mya asked with an attitude as she entered her apartment. "Oh excuse my mess. I intended to put them up, but as you can see, I got distracted."

Janiece's eyes got big. Piles of clothes were in the middle of the floor. "Okay."

"Put your stuff in that back bedroom on the left," Mya tossed out before the telephone rang.

She stared as Mya stepped over the clothes to answer the phone that was on two wooden crates that served as her coffee table. Surveying her surroundings, Janiece noticed unwashed dishes in the sink and things left out on the countertop to the left side of the apartment. She rolled her eyes as she walked down the hallway. She opened the

28

door and gasped. The room was messier than the living room. A twin size bed, with a worn-out comforter and mixed-matched pillowcases. She threw her bags on the floor. Maybe I shoulda stayed home. It's nasty here, she thought as she closed the door. She strolled back to where Mya was and she was still cackling on the phone.

"Girl, let me call you back," Mya said as she hung up the phone. "Oh, there are rules you have to abide by if you staying here."

Janiece eyed Mya as she sat on the sofa. "Like what."

"Rule one: We don't share men. Rule two: My money is my money. Rule three: When you get a job, you gotta pay something around here like groceries or the water bill. Rule four: And what is done here don't leave this apartment," she stated. "Girl, I'm just tryin' to protect you 'cause I ain't never had no sister and you come close. I mean you grown now since you wanna leave home at seventeen and shit. Ya feel me," Mya uttered as she extended her hand.

Janiece shook her hand. She didn't quite understand what she was agreeing to. She felt like this was a big change for her. It felt good. A place to grow. Freedom is what she really wanted.

Glancing at the rest of the living room, she saw that Mya had pictures of family on the walls and wooden crates. One particular picture caught her eye. It was a picture of a man. It made her consider did she want to live here or not. Would she feel comfortable having Mya's man gawk at her? Would her clothing bring attention? Would she and Mya get into it because of him? In the back of her mind, she could hear her grandma's voice, 'Don't be wearin' dem short shorts. Them men's' be thinking the worse of you young girls. You don't want to cause extra attention, 'Neece.'

Later on that day

Janiece strolled from her room and into the living room where a man was lying on the sofa. It was the same man from the picture. He was dark-skinned, his skin the texture of driftwood, rough around the edges with a deep copper undertone. He had cornrows and a long, unkempt beard. His right hand was in his boxer shorts. One leg on the sofa and the other one barely touching the floor. He stirred in his sleep but didn't wake up.

She tiptoed into the kitchen and saw an empty pizza box, on the floor with baby roaches nibbling on it.

"Eww," she said.

She turned on the light and the roaches scattered away. The trash was packed to the top and some onto the floor. She opened the refrigerator and saw nothing she wanted to eat because the roaches turned her stomach. Just then, she felt a presence behind her. She turned around and was startled. The man from the sofa was watching her. She closed the refrigerator.

"Who you?" he asked with a mischievous smile and showing his gold grill with his right hand still in his pants fumbling around his manhood.

"I'm Janiece, Mya's friend. I hope she told you that I will be here for a while," she answered not looking down where his right hand was.

"Yeah she did," he said. "Oh, don't mind me."

Janiece smiled and walked out of the kitchen and into her room. She closed the door behind her and locked it.

Soon as she sat down on the twin size bed, she heard heavy footsteps.

Knock. Knock.

"Who is it?"

"It's Derrell."

She swung open the door, "Yeah."

"Come out for a minute."

Oh gosh, what does he want? She stepped out and he was dressed in jeans, a brown Polo shirt, and Polo boots.

"If you don't mind, can you clean up this mess for me while I step out? I don't want Mya to be complainin' about the mess I made here," he said pointing to the bedroom he and Mya shared.

Janiece looked past him into their bedroom before returning her scowl to him. He handed her twenty dollars. She glared at the money and jerked her neck back. He didn't wait for a response as he walked away. Folding her arms over her chest, she fumed on the inside. Dang, I left one household for another to be cleanin' up other people's mess.

She regarded his smug walk. After hearing the door

shut, she walked the few steps across the hall and stared at the mess she was forced to clean up. There were empty beer bottles on the floor. Some on the bed. Clothes were everywhere. Used condoms scattered on the floor. Before doing anything, she left the bedroom and stepped inside the hall bathroom. She hoped to find some gloves. Thank God she did because there was no way she was going to use her bare hands to clean up their nasty room.

She spent the next twenty minutes cleaning. As she piled the dirty clothes into a corner, she thought, I'm a whole maid out chea cleanin' up after grown folks. I thought Mya said I was like a sister to her. I mean, I don't mind helpin' but I ain't about to be y'all maid, the entire time I stay here.

When Mya entered her apartment, she saw Janiece sitting on the sofa. She sauntered to her bedroom as she recalled the text messages with her boyfriend.

Derrell: Aye, yo' girl is kinda hot. Her light-skinned ass and them freckles. I ain't know black people get freckles yo'. She's too skinny for my taste tho'. Maybe she'll be good for my dawg. Go ahead and show her the ropes of the game.

Mya: Yeah, I was thinkin' about that. Let me break her in first before we hand her over to yo' boy. Dang, she just moved in with me.

Derrell: Aight bet.

Mya: Yeah, she's one of them young and easy to train types that will do anything for some change.

Derrell: Like you?

Mya: Whatever!

Mya hated being compared to other females. It made her feel unworthy. Not attractive enough. Self-conscious to the next woman. It irked her nerves but knowing what Derrell had done for her. She put on her big girl panties and brushed off his snide remarks. Even though it hurt her feelings. She felt like Janiece was coming in between her and Derrell and must show her the ropes soon. She had to put the plan in motion.

"My man told me you cleaned up the room for twenty dollars. He fine ain't he?"

"He's all right," was all Janiece replied.

34

Mya jerked her neck back and smacked her lips. "You don't think my man fine? What he too dark for you? You only date light-skinned brothas and white boys?" she asked in a nasty attitude, eyeing Janiece up and down. "I hope you don't think just because you light-skinned mean that you're better than me."

"I don't think that at all. I was just—" Janiece said springing to her feet in defense.

Mya tossed her long burgundy braids over her shoulder. "I hope not because I grew up believing I wasn't good enough because of the color of my skin. My mama found no fault in my brother because he was lighter than me. She had this thing if a person was light meant they were gon' to go far in life. That shit crazy, ain't it? Did you ever have to go through that with your peoples?"

"Yeah, my grandma judged me a lot. She would comment on the sly that my mama didn't know who my father was because she was out there doin' only God knows what because I'm lighter than my mama. But my grandpa is light-skinned himself. So I don't know if it was a color thing or not but it seemed like she did everything she could to bring me down."

"Yeah I know right. Growing up in these toxic ass homes." Mya snickered. "Well in this household there ain't no color barrier. We all the same."

"I agree with you 100%."

"Hey, remember you told me you were a virgin. You still one?" she asked as she saw Janiece nod her head. "I got peoples if you thought of losin' your virginity since you grown and shit." She laughed.

"Thanks but no thanks. I'm gonna save myself for my husband one day. No offense, I have standards. I ain't tryna be out here givin' my cat to every Tom, Dick, and Harry as my grandma would say," she chortled in a low tone.

Mya cocked her neck and sneered at her. Man, you ain't even got a pot to piss in, you judgmental bitch! At this moment, she despised Janiece. How could someone past judgment and be homeless at the same time? A slight chuckle escaped her lips.

"Well, you ain't gotta say it like that, dang girl.

Everybody can't be like you. So just because I lost my virginity at sixteen make me a hoe?"

Janiece instantly shook her head.

Mya scowled at her for several minutes and then burst out laughing. "Girl, I'm just messin' with you. Yo face was hilarious."

Janiece found nothing funny as she stared at her friend. Her inner voice asked her, 'Are you sure you wanna live with Mya?' Putting on a fake smile, the corner of her mouth lifted an inch. "Haha. What're you getting into today?"

"Ain't no I. It's we. We're gon' hit the club tonight so you gotta be fly." Mya paused. "I'm gon' show you the ropes on how to reel in a man."

"I didn't say I wanted a man," Janiece replied.

Mya paused and snapped. "Sis, since you ain't bringing in no paper right now, I got to show you how to get paid."

"Ugh, don't you work tomorrow?"

"Yeah. So." Mya rolled her eyes and swung her hair around.

"It's not gonna mess you up in the mornin'?"

"Girl, I am not about to be arguin' cause we gon' to the club tonight."

"Yeah I guess I'm gon' then," Janiece said in agreement. "This time I'll be fly."

"Whatever. You ain't gonna be as fly as me. You can't outshine me 'cause you stayin' wit me. You wouldn't want me to throw you out 'cause you getting all the attention," Mya stated, throwing shade as she eyed Janiece.

"It shouldn't matter to you no way. You got a man."

Mya snickered. "What he don't know won't hurt him."

Chapter 3

Enter through the narrow gate, for wide is the gate and broad is the road that leads to destruction. Matthew 7:13.

Janiece

Saturday morning

Janiece was dogged tired from coming in the apartment hours ago. So when she opened her eyes, she expected quietness, and not this loud, thumping music. She lay awake and stared at the ceiling. She rubbed her eyes, looked at the clock on the wooden crate that served as a nightstand, and saw that it was three in the morning.

"Do these people ever go to sleep?" she mumbled.

Just then, she had to tinkle. She sat up in bed and looked towards the door. She threw back the sheets and climbed out the bed. As she strode near the door, she heard knocking on it. She jumped, halting her steps in place. The knocking increased rapidly and steadily then abruptly stopped. The fear caught in her chest. Knowing someone could be lurking at her door. All she wanted to do was pee in peace.

Standing by the door, Janiece put her ear against it to listen for sounds next to her door. When she didn't hear anything, she opened the door and tiptoed toward the bathroom when a guy appeared out of nowhere and startled her.

"Hey, pretty lady."

Hand covering her heart, she reacted. "You scared me."

He licked his lips. "My bad shawty. You look good tonight. Why you ain't out here chillin' with us?"

She wanted to answer him but she had to pee. She pushed past him and entered the bathroom. Still sleepy and hoping that guy would be gone, she opened the door and he was leaning on the door frame.

"Say shawty, you got a man?" he asked, standing taller than what he appeared before.

She shook her head and tried to rush passed him but he caught her by the arm and spun her around before she could reach her room.

"Why you runnin' shawty? You gonna tell me your name or do I have to keep callin' you shawty?" he asked, flashing a gold grill in his mouth. "Shawty."

Janiece wasn't in the mood. She jerked her arm from his grasp. She eyeballed him up and down with an irritated look across her face. Rolling her eyes nonstop had her agitated because he was pissing her off. All she wanted to do was jump in bed, block off the head-splitting music, and go back to sleep.

He grabbed for her arms and she shrugged away. "My bad shawty. So whatchu sayin'?"

"Boy, leave my girl alone," she heard Mya say and was thankful she saved her in the nick of time. "What're you don' up?"

Janiece faced Mya. "Uh, I had to pee."

"Yeah right. You know you wanted to see what all this noise was about. I told you we party constantly. You either get addicted or hate it," Mya announced. "So are you gonna stay up with us?"

"Who's all in there?" Janiece asked in a groggy voice.

"My home girls, my man and some of his friends and

some other girls. You can join us if you want."

"What're y'all don'?"

"You askin' too many questions. Come find out," was all Mya said before disappearing into the living room.

Janiece contemplated going into the living room but she declined and went into her bedroom hoping to block out the noise. It didn't do her any good because the party lasted way in the morning so she tossed and turned all night.

Saturday evening while Janiece was sitting on the sofa watching television. She noticed out of the corner of her eyes as Mya and her boyfriend Derrell entered the house. They carried liquor and beer in grocery bags. They didn't speak as they entered the apartment but went straight into the kitchen and placed the bags on the counter.

"Hey girl, you wanna get a taste of this?" asked Mya, placing the liquor bottles on top of the table.

Janiece spun her head toward the kitchen. "No, what is it?"

"Some Cîroc Vodka, Pirate Bay Rum, Smirnoff, E &

J, and some Coors light."

"You actually drink that stuff?" Janiece asked with a bewildered expression.

"Duh girl!" Mya said as she stuck the Cîroc and Smirnoff in the freezer and the other liquor and beer in the refrigerator.

"Where's the food?"

Mya shouted, "At the store!"

Janiece frowned. "Why y'all bought all that liquor and no food? I'm starvin'."

Becoming annoyed by questions, Mya flipped. "I thought you were gonna look for a job. You lied to me. I am not the only one who eats here."

"My bad, danggg."

"Yeah, it is your bad. Just because you left home don't mean I'm gonna take care of you. This is the real world. You gotta do for you, 'Lil sis. So when are you gon' job huntin'?"

"I'll go tomorrow."

"Yeah keep sayin' that. If you don't find a job real soon then you might be out on the streets. I don't take care of no grown woman."

"I'm not grown," she uttered, her voice weak.

"Well you shoulda stayed your ass home."

Janiece's feelings were bruised. She got up and left as she entered her bedroom. Her anger was boiling right now as she stood in the middle of the room. Her shoulders heaved up and down. Her breathing hard and fist balled at her waist. How could Mya treat her with no respect? Before, Mya told her that she was like a sister but she lied. Not wanting to mingle with them, she stayed inside her bedroom for the next two hours. She pondered maybe staying with her ridiculing Grandma would have been better instead of here.

It wasn't ten o clock at night yet when noisy chatter and laughter echoed from the living room. She tossed over in bed. She began to watch a show on the small portable TV that rested on a cherry top dresser. That was the only decent furniture in the room. She glanced around the room in shame. A crate served as a nightstand, sheets served as curtains for the one window in the room and a closet door that hung off its hinges. As she stared at the

TV show, her mind began wandering again.

She questioned how come the landlord or their next-door neighbors never complained about loud noises, folks partying and loudmouthed people dancing. All of what she wished she could be doing at the moment but instead she was crying. Crying for her mama. Crying for her Grandparents. Crying for herself. She hadn't wept since that morning she rode in th car with Mya. She later learned she OD'd off of cocaine. The one killer that her mama swore she wouldn't touch. But her mama lied. Lied to not only her but herself as well because now she is gone and in the earth. She cried long and hard, hoping the pain would go away. For a moment, she thought the pain won but realized she was sleepy from all the sobbing. Suddenly her eyelids closed and sleep fell upon her.

Hours later

Janiece's body jerked to the ongoing laughter and music. She cracked her eyes open. Feeling tired from crying earlier, she hoped the sadness would leave. But it was still there. Depression was her new best friend.

45

Having a sense of giving up and forgetting the past, she got up from the bed and walked toward the door. She pulled open the door. She stuck her head out and caught a glimpse of the folks in the living room. Rushing inside the bathroom, she flushed her face with cool water. She tried to erase the redness out of her eyes. Turning off the water, she grabbed a face towel and dried her face. Turning over a new leaf in her life, she had to be presentable if this was going to be her life. She lifted her head and stared at the person in the mirror. A soft cry caught in her throat. She shook her head. This is the new you, embrace it, she thought as she exited the bathroom. Soon as she walked up the hall, the voices stopped and heads faced her.

"Heyyy girl. Glad you could make it," Mya said turning to face her after gnawing on Derrell's neck.

Janiece nodded and stared straight ahead.

The same guy from last night pulled a chair from the kitchen table, placed it by the sofa and motioned for her to take a seat. Janiece accepted the invitation and sat in the chair.

"Sup shawty, what can I get you?"

"Anything."

He arched his eyebrows. "You sure?"

She nodded.

"What should I get your girl to drink?" he asked Mya.

"She's a virgin."

Janiece's eyes bulged as she glared at Mya with stone-cold eyes. The guy smiled and nodded his head.

"I meant her drink. Mix her drink with Sprite and a 'Lil Cîroc," Mya hollered. "My bad," she mouthed back at her.

"All right," he said as he left to fill up her cup.

It didn't take him long to come back with an eight-ounce cup and a beer in his left hand. "So shawty, what's yo name?"

"Janiece."

"Since you didn't ask, I'm Breezy."

She didn't. She held the cup up to her nose, smelled it, and scrunched up her nose.

"What's wrong shawty, it's too strong for ya?"

"No, I wanted to smell it first before I drank it."

"Well go ahead and take a sip ma'," he said.

She put the cup up to her mouth to swallow the liquid. She let out a screeching sound because it was strong. She heard laughter and figured it was directed at her.

By the end of the night, Janiece had tasted every bottle of liquor in the apartment, straight up and mixed. She didn't care anymore because she was free and her mama was gone.

Chapter 4

Love is patient, love is kind...it's not easily angered...1 Corinthians 13:4-5.

Janiece

"Get up Janiece! You got to find a job today," she heard a voice vibrate somewhere nearby.

"Janiece, get up."

She wanted to wake up but couldn't figure out who was calling her. Just then, she felt pressure on her arm. A shaking and pushing sensation. She turned in the direction of the force and she opened her eyes to Mya standing above her. "Where am I?"

"In your bed."

"What time is it?" asked Janiece, blinking her eyes open and closed.

"It's two in the evening."

Her head pounded. Janiece moaned, "What day is it?"

Mya shook her arm and said, "Girl stop playin'. You know its Sunday afternoon," she chuckled. "That's what happens when you think you're grown."

"My head hurts. I don't think I can look for a job today. I need to lie in bed 'til I feel better."

"Whatever! You're getting out the bed today. That's called a hangover by the way." Mya stepped backward. "I'll go get you two Ibuprofen and then you got to get up and find a job."

Upon hearing footsteps and an aggravating voice above her, Janiece glanced over at Mya's stretched out hands. "Where's the water?" she asked as she grabbed the pills.

Mya picked up a cup off the floor and walked out of the room. "Here."

"Is that the bathroom water?"

"Yeah. Ain't nothing wrong with the bathroom water. We drink it all the time."

Janiece lazily sat up in bed. It felt like the room was spinning. Her headache was painful. She swallowed the pills with lukewarm tap water. She set the cup down on the crate and fell back onto the pillows.

"Uh uh, you got to get up today and find a job," Mya started pulling on her arm. "It's not my fault that you got drunk. When I get off of work tonight, I better see some job applications on the table," Mya retorted in an exasperated tone as she walked out the door.

Janiece got out of bed three hours later. She knew Mya didn't get off work until eight so there was no need to rush. Dressed in jeans, a dressy shirt, and black flats, she strode down the hallway. The sight before her eyes disgusted her. The living room was a hot mess. She spotted crushed chips on the sofa, cups were thrown on the floor and empty food containers left on top of the table. She shook her head and realized she didn't have a spare key. She backtracked and entered Mya's room but to her amazement, there were clothes everywhere, empty beer bottles on the floor, and empty condom wrappers again. Oh no, I am not cleaning this up this time, she mused as she stepped across the clothes to retrieve the key off Mya's dresser. Once she seized it, she hurried from the room, grabbed a light jacket and purse from her room and walked outside, shutting the door behind her. She walked to the nearest bus stop. That was how she got around unless she rode with Mya somewhere.

Janiece walked down the street onto North Greenwood Street and stood next to an older, middle-aged woman who wore pink curlers in her hair. There was also a young, brown skin guy with dreads that hung past his shoulders. The guy made eye contact with her and said what's up with the nodding of his head. She smiled back. The screeching of tires made her look up to see the bus. The doors opened. The woman got on first, then she and then the guy.

Janiece deposited the coins in the container and walked to the middle of the bus and sat on the left-hand side. The guy who was standing at the bus stop sat a couple of seats behind her. The bus driver closed her doors and proceeded its journey to LaGrange Mall.

Quietness was what she wanted.

"Spp, spp."

"Spp, spp," she heard the noise again.

She saw a young Hispanic girl who sat across from her laugh. The girl tossed her wavy, black hair back and chuckled loudly.

"Spp, spp," a male's voice said.

Janiece concentrated on the ride to the mall. She wanted to ignore whoever was trying to get her attention. She glanced at the Hispanic girl and she burst out in a deep laugh.

"Can't you see she's ignorin' you?" the girl said.

"What's yo' name shawty?" the guy asked from behind her seat.

"Janiece."

"Sup Janiece, I'm Jakeem," he stuck out his hand.

She glanced down at his hands. Shook them and hoped he went back to his seat. Just then she was saved by the bell when the girl jumped to her rescue.

"Obviously, she doesn't want you to bother her, Jakeem. Leave her alone before I tell her about you," she said with sass as she twisted her neck side to side.

"Shut up Jennifer, who made you the boss?" Jakeem asked as he hunched his shoulders and moved away.

She was thankful for the girl speaking up for her. But she didn't want to engage in small talk with her either. The rest of the bus ride was smooth. As soon as the bus pulled up to the curve, Janiece leaped to her feet. She marched off the bus.

"Wait up."

Oh gosh, not today. All I want is a job, she thought. Janiece didn't turn around but rather felt a hand on her right shoulder.

"Hey, hold up for a minute." The girl stopped her and stuck out her hand. "I'm Jennifer. You don't have to worry about Jakeem botherin' you. He messes with all the new girls on the bus."

"Thanks," replied Janiece.

Walking with a small knockoff Coach purse glued to her shoulder, Jennifer asked, "How old are you?"

"Seventeen."

"Really? You look older."

Janiece had hoped once they entered the mall that Jennifer would go her separate way. Unfortunately, she stayed with her until her job hunt was over.

"Hey, you wanna stop in Goody's?"

"Nah, that'll be my last spot," Janiece said so she could ask Mya for a ride later.

It was close to eight o'clock when Janiece told her

that she was going to catch a ride with her friend Mya.

"You want me to wait for you to make sure you get a ride home? You know the bus don't come back 'til nine."

"I'm cool."

"You sure?" Jennifer asked with a sincere heart.

"Yeah I'm cool," Janiece said as she walked into Goody's, leaving Jennifer standing in 579, a store for the young and hip women.

"Okay, I guess I'll see you around."

Janiece walked into Goody's carrying four applications that she got from Claire's, Belk's, Bath and Body Works, and 579's. Her friend Mya had never told her what department she worked in so Janiece walked around in the small store looking for her. Five minutes had passed when she walked up to an average height, blonde woman standing behind the counter. She asked for Mya but the woman told her that Mya didn't show up for work.

Frustrated and disappointed, Janiece walked out of Goody's. She looked down at her watch and she still had a lot of time before she got back on the bus. So she walked to the food court and ordered a hamburger, fries and a drink. She found a seat and sat down at the many tables providing for the eateries in the food court. Slurping Mountain Dew through her straw, she heard a familiar voice.

"Guess your friend left early," Jennifer said and sat down at the table inviting herself without being asked.

"No, she didn't even work tonight," she answered annoyed.

"Damn, that's messed up. She had you thinkin' she was workin' and all," she said. "Why you out here by yourself in the first place? If she was a true friend then she would have dropped you off and went about her business. She got to know that there are crazy people that ride the bus."

She cut her eyes at Jennifer and questioned, "Why do you ride the bus? Are you crazy?"

Jennifer laughed. "No, I'm not crazy but I can act crazy so folks won't bother me. Like Jakeem, he knows not to mess with me. I joke a 'Lil and then he knows what's up. Yeah, you're still naïve. How old did you say you were again?"

"Seventeen," Janiece answered. "How old are you?"

"How old do I look?"

Janiece shrugged her shoulders, "I don't know; maybe nineteen."

"You're correct." Jennifer glanced down at her Timex watch and suggested they returned to the bus stop.

The bus pulled up seconds later. Janiece stepped on the bus and sat on the same side but in a different seat. Just her luck, Jennifer sat across from her.

"If you don't mind me asking, aren't you like in the eleventh grade, right?"

"I was but I dropped out. End of story and I don't want to talk about it. Let's talk about you."

Jennifer threw her hands in the air. "Okay. Okay. Touchy subject." Jennifer scooted closer to the edge of the seat. "So what'd you wanna know?"

"I don't know and don't care."

Jennifer smirked but answered, "Since you're so interested, I live at home with my mami and two brothers. Unlike your friend you talked about, I have and keep my job. I work at Los Naples on Vernon road. You know where that is, don't you?" Los Naples consisted of Italian food.

"Yeah. Are y'all hiring?" asked Janiece.

"Not at the moment but you want my number just in case?" Jennifer muttered as the bus came to a stop.

Janiece rolled her eyes. "I guess."

Jennifer instantly stood up and asked a man for a pen. She walked up to Janiece and jotted down her number on top of one of her applications. "I'll see you around."

Janiece said goodbye and walked off the bus.

Chapter 5

*Enter not into the path of the wicked and go not in the
way of evil. Proverbs 4:14.*

Janiece

Janiece climbed the second floor of the complex. She
inserted her key and entered, finding Mya and Derrell
getting it on. She frowned at her friend in a tank top and
boy-shorts on. They didn't stop what they were doing.
Janiece lifted her lip in disgust.

"Hey girl, where you been? I've been lookin' for
you," Mya said, tossing over her shoulder.

Janiece shut and locked the door behind her.
"Obviously, you didn't try hard enough," she mumbled as
she walked into the hallway that led to her room.

She heard Derrell mumble something to Mya before
she burst out laughing. "What you got there?"

"Applications, didn't you ask me to do that?"

She entered the room and took off her shoes. She
placed them under the bed. She exited her room and
caught them in the same position that she had seen them

in seconds ago. She stepped inside the kitchen. She opened the refrigerator and saw different brands of beer, liquor, and Chinese food.

"Whose food is this?"

Mya hollered. "It's for the party tonight."

"Another one," she mumbled softly.

"What'd you say?" Mya asked.

"Nothing," she answered as she grabbed a cup and turned on the cold water from the faucet. "What time did you get off tonight?"

Mya stopped chuckling. "What you questionin' me now?"

"No, I just asked. I went by your job."

Mya lifted herself off of Derrell's lap and looked into the kitchen toward her. "Bitch, you checkin' on me?"

Appalled by her outburst, Janiece stared at Mya for a brief second and glanced away to turn off the faucet.

"You didn't do what I think you did, did you?"

"I was lookin' for a ride home, that's all. I didn't mean anything by it."

"Girl, I hope they ain't gonna fire me. That's my third

time callin' out this week," Mya uttered.

The sisterly feelings for Mya were slowly dying. Janiece clutched the cup of water and stormed out of the kitchen. It was becoming a routine for Mya to go off on her. It wasn't like she could cuss her out. If she did, she knew she would be out on the streets. She had to suck it up and keep it moving.

"You ain't gonna watch TV with us?" she heard the sarcasm in Derrell's voice as she walked passed him.

She didn't glance in his direction. She kept walking until she reached her door. When she entered the room, she locked it and turned on the TV manually because the remote didn't work. She climbed in bed after taking a few sips of water.

Hours later, she heard music.

Thump. Thump.

Snap yo' Fingers by T-Pain blasted through the walls as Janiece lay across the bed watching The Parkers. Just then she remembered she had Jennifer's number. She reached for the first application with the number on it and picked it up. Since there wasn't a phone in the room, she knew she had to go out of the room to get the cordless phone from Mya's bedroom. She opened the door while Magic Stick by Lil Kim played next. She hoped that she wouldn't run into anybody as she retrieved the phone.

She sprinted across to Mya's bedroom. She opened the door and was surprised because it looked like somebody tried to clean up but there were clothes still on the floor. She grabbed the cordless phone that was lying on the ironing board. The door creaked and she spun around. Derrell occupied the doorway as he gave her a smug look.

She raised the phone in the air, stuttering. "I...I came to get the phone, that's all."

He didn't say anything as he watched her. She dashed by him. Once she made it into the room, she locked the door and jumped on the bed. She hit the green 'talk' button to make sure no one was on the phone and before dialing Jennifer's number.

"Hola," a Hispanic woman answered.

Janiece figured the woman probably didn't speak English so the little Spanish she learned from high school came in handy. "Hola, como estas? Puedo hablar con Jennifer?" (Hello, how're you? Can I speak to Jennifer?)

The woman said something and then she said, "Jennifer?"

"Si," she answered as she heard the phone being laid down and Spanish speaking in the background.

Within seconds, Jennifer said, "Hello."

"Hey Jennifer, this is Janiece."

"Yeah, I know. What're you up to?" asked Jennifer.

"Nothing much just watchin' TV."

"What's all that music?"

She sat crossed leg and answered, "Oh, my friend havin' a party."

"Why are you not in there?"

"I don't feel like it." Janiece uncrossed her legs. "What're you up to tonight?"

"Gon' to a salsa club."

"Oh."

"You sound bored. I don't see how when there's a party gon' on," Jennifer said. "Could you understand mi Madre?"

"Yeah just hola and Jennifer."

Jennifer giggled. "Mi Madre speaks a little English but the rest of us can speak it pretty well."

"Your mom sounds sweet," replied Janiece.

"Thanks, she is. She works at the Best Western hotel don' housekeeping. You wanna come over?"

Janiece thought, anywhere but here for a while. "I thought you were gon' to the salsa club. I don't want to ruin your night."

"Girl, you ain't don' nothing. So you comin'?"

"You sure?" asked Janiece, not wanting to ruin Jennifer's night.

"Yeah. You know where Adamson and Maple Street is?"

"Yeah, that's not far from my grandparents' house," Janiece answered in a contrite tone.

"Really? That is so cool."

"Yeah," was all she said.

"Well, I stay on Maple Street. The fourth house down on the right side in a greenhouse. Don't forget what I said about the bus. You gotta act hard so dey don't mess with you."

"Okay, I'll see you in thirty minutes," was all she said. She changed into skin-tight jeans, black heels and a tube top with a light jacket covering her arms. She grasped her bus pass and sauntered outside without being stopped by anyone.

She marched to the nearest bus stop. The bus didn't take long to arrive. She got on the bus and sat in the middle, peering out the window. Her ride to Jennifer's only took ten minutes. She exited the bus and walked the few steps to Jennifer's house. She knocked on the door.

"Who is it?" a child's voice asked.

"It's Janiece."

"Who?" the childlike voice asked again.

"Jennifer's friend," she said as she heard voices on the other side and then the door opened.

"Hey girl, come on in," she said in her Spanish accent. "This is my Madre, Lupita, and my siblings."

Janiece stared at the five-foot, dark curly-haired woman. Her mama caught her off guard by hugging her. She couldn't do anything but hug her back.

"Okay mami, we gon' in the back," Jennifer said in Spanish. Unlike Mya's apartment, Jennifer's family had decent furniture. They had a real coffee table, end tables, and plants to lighten up the atmosphere. Jennifer and Janiece went to a club called Baia Chicos. It was a mixed environment with various music ranging from techno, house music, and Spanish music. Hours later after Janiece walked into Mya's apartment, the party was still going. This was their routine, drinking and partying almost every day of the week. It carried on for the next month nonstop.

Chapter 6

Stay away from a foolish man, for you will not find knowledge on his lips. Proverbs 19:27.

Janiece

Night after night turned into a month later. It was hot as hell in June. They sauntered inside the club at ten at night. Mya nudged her on the arm and told her that she was going to find her a man tonight. Janiece didn't object. She got herself into this world and so she had to abide by it or go home. Janiece looked over Mya's attire and she was fly as hell. She looked down at her outfit and was just as fly as her homegirl. Mya found them a table. Her friend began schooling her on how to catch a paid man.

"Janiece, you gotta stop being so naïve when it comes to these little boys out here. To get you a balla, he gotta have a job. I don't care if he is a dope boy. He gotta wear jewelry; that means he got dough. You got to look at what they're wearin'. I mean how you supposed to get paid if you hookin' up with a guy with dirty shoes on? Just because a guy is cute don't mean he got that paper." Mya demonstrated by rubbing her fingertips together. "Sometimes you need an ugly mofo to get that bread. And you gotta know how to work your goods to get what you want."

Janiece heard her friend alright but she asked anyway. "You work your goods when you have Derrell?"

Shock registered on Mya's face; she could tell. Mya's caramel complexion darkened. "Bitch do as I say," Mya snapped before sauntering away in the crowd.

Janiece knew it was going to be a long night so she might as well start tonight. Guys after guys came toward the table and asked her to dance. She dismissed two guys because of their shoes. One guy because he wasn't wearing enough gold around his neck and another guy because he wasn't hood enough.

She glanced around the club until she found Mya hugged up in the corner with a lanky guy with braids. She shook her head. She bobbed her head along to Saltshaker by YingYang Twins. The music switched to a Lil Kim song as she sang along to the fast rhythm of music.

A tall light-skinned guy wearing a du-rag stopped in

front of her table. "Sup shawty, I've been watchin' you for a long time."

She eyed him up and down. He appeared thuggish like. He had on baggy pants with a gold ring on his index finger.

"Do you mind if I sit down?" he asked in a deep tone.

Janiece shook her head. She watched as the guy sat down next to her. "So Lil' mama, how old are you?"

"Seventeen and you?"

"I'm nineteen. I'm Demarius but my boys call me D-money. What's your name?" he asked, scooting closer to her.

Janiece ogled the guy next to her. She leaned forward and inhaled his earthy scent. "I'm Janiece," she said clearing her throat.

He faced her. "You good ma'?"

"My throat is scratchy. Do you think you could get me something to drink?"

"Yeah, I got you. Anything you want in particular?"

"Amaretto Sour," she stated as she watched him get up and walked toward the bar. When he returned minutes later, he handed the drink to her.

"Thanks, what're you drinkin' on?"

"Shit, Bud Light on draft," he sipped the bottle. "So tell me why you sitting down and not dancin' with your fine ass?"

"Because I ain't got nobody to dance with unless you're willin' to dance."

"Nah, I don't dance but we can hang out sometime if you like."

"That's cool," she stated. She saw Mya walking in her direction. "I'll give you my home girl number. That's the number you can reach me if you really wanna holla."

"Aiight bet," he said as he stood up from the table and walked off.

Soon as D-money left, she saw Mya stomped toward her table in a drunken state she assumed as the way she was staggering.

"You ready?" Mya asked in a slur.

Yep, she's drunk. "Been ready," was all Janiece said as she followed Mya outside the club.

Monday evening

She received a phone call when Mya told her to pick up the phone. She yelled "You need to teach him some manners!"

Janiece was excited that D-money called. She didn't want to appear too anxious so she took deep breaths before saying hello.

"Hey, what's up?"

"Nothing much. You?"

"Chillin'. What's up with yo' girl? Female got mad problems," he voiced as she laughed because that was the same thing Mya said about him.

"So whatchu' wanna get into tonight?"

Janiece sighed because she was tired of going clubbing with Mya. For a change, she wanted to kick back at the apartment and chill. "You want to come over to my place?"

"Fo sho'. Is yo' girl gon' to be there?" he asked annoyed.

"Yeah."

"Umm, how about you come to my place instead?"

"Where do you live?"

She heard the excitement in his voice that she agreed to come over to his place. It was the first time they had talked on the phone since meeting him at the club last night.

"I live on Highland Avenue in a white house. It has a blue truck in the front yard. So you comin'?"

"What're we gonna do?" she asked, nervously.

"Watch a few movies and enjoy each other's company."

"Okay, I'll see you in an hour."

Dressed in a pink shirt, brown shorts, and pink sandals, Janiece walked out of her room carrying a small black purse clutched to her shoulder. She first went into the kitchen to grab something to drink. Soon as she walked out of the kitchen, Mya appeared in the hallway.

"Where you gon'?"

"Gon' over my friend's house," Janiece said hurriedly to get out the door.

"Wait, hold up," Mya stated as she glared at her walking behind the TV. She grabbed something and then tossed the object at her.

Janiece stepped out the way. Her eyes landed on the foil wrapper on the floor. "Why you throw that at me?"

"You're gonna need it for protection."

Grimacing at Mya, Janiece stated, "I'm not gon' to do anything with him."

"Yeah, that's what you think. Just be careful," Mya voiced as she walked back down the hallway.

Walking through the neighborhood to cut across Highland Avenue, Janiece heard grown and young men whistle as she cut through the yards. She paid them no mind. The only person she was looking forward to was D-money. She knew after just meeting him, he seemed like a cool dude to hang with. So she was too excited when he called her today. As Janiece turned the corner of the street, she spied a white house with a blue truck and a red car in the yard.

I hope this is his yard. I need to get me a phone, she thought. Janiece walked up to the house and knocked on the door. A tall, brown skin man came to the door. "How can I help you?" he asked as if he was going somewhere in a hurry.

"I'm here to see D-money."

The man smiled and then hollered into the house for Demarius. Demarius came up front. The man turned toward him and said, "Ain't nothin' gon' to happen in my house while I'm gone. I'll be back."

"Dad, you're a trip," D-money said as his dad looked back at him with a stern look and walked out the house, leaving the door open.

"Sup, my dad's a trip. You can come in," D-money announced to her as she slid inside the house.

Janiece stepped into the house and glanced at her surroundings. The furniture looked tidy. It had a sofa and a matching love seat with a brown leather bench as the coffee table. The house had many pictures on the walls and plants scattered throughout the house. It looked like someone lived and took care of the home. As soon as D-money led her into his room, it was like she stepped inside of a teen's room. He had a twin-size bed. A closet was full of jerseys and basketball shoes. A basket of clothes in the corner of his room. A twenty-seven-inch

TV with a DVD player and a stereo. And lots of magazines on the floor.

"Have a seat, would you like something to drink?"

"Sure," was all she said.

Her eyes followed as he suddenly returned with a glass of red Kool-Aid. He had a small cup for himself also. As she drunk from the glass, he flipped the channel to 106 and Park, a BET show as she sat on the edge of the twin-size bed. Janiece sat uncomfortably, crossing and uncrossing her legs. She glared over at D-money and he cracked a smile.

"What're you smiling' about?"

"I was thinkin' about something," he answered. "You wanna watch a movie?"

"Sure."

D-money stood up from the bed and walked toward his game console. He lifted the top of the PlayStation 2. Then he rummaged through a stack of DVDs in a box that was located underneath the TV. He quickly took out a movie and popped it in without asking her if she liked the movie. He flipped the channel to input one and turned on the power of the game system. Then he picked up the remote of the game and fast-forwarded through the previews.

"What movie is this?" Janiece asked with curiosity.

"National Treasure. You ever seen it?" he asked with his back to her.

"Yeah," she stated.

"You can lean back against the wall if you want," he said scooting himself against the wall.

Janiece didn't move.

"Aye, you can sit back with me. I ain't gonna bite unless you want me too," he chuckled lightly.

Leaving no choice but to slip out of her sandals and scoot back, Janiece obliged. Toward the middle of the movie, she caught D-money staring at her a few times but it didn't bother her. During the scene where Nicholas Cage stole the Declaration from the museum, D-money stretched his arms over her head and laid his left arm around her neck. She thought it was cute so she leaned in closer.

While engrossed in the movie, D-money slightly

touched her on her thigh and she jumped. "What're you don'?" she asked in a nervous voice, eyeing him suspiciously as he licked his lips.

His hands shot up in the air. "My bad shawty. I was rubbin' the scar on your leg. How did you get that?"

She answered tensely, "I got that when I was ridin' my bike with a couple of friends to the corner store," she answered self-consciously. "I turned the curb too fast, hit the curb and flipped, landing on top of my bike."

"Does it hurt still?"

She shook her head.

"I only asked because I got a scar and every now and then it still hurts," he said pointing to a scar on his left foot. "Can I touch it? I mean to see if it still hurt you?" he asked appearing with a puppy dog expression.

Janiece shook her head yes.

D-money softly touched the scar and then pushed it harder. He asked her did it hurt when he put pressure on it and she shook her head no again. He kept his hand on her thigh and started making small circles around the scar. She elbowed him in the side when she told him to pay

77

attention to the movie. He looked at her with his hand still on her thigh.

"Okay, okay I'll watch it," he mused as his hand started upward.

Janiece didn't care at first. She wanted to see how far he would try to go without her interrupting him. He inched closer and was at the rim of her shorts when she pushed his hand away.

"I wasn't gon' to do nothing," he whispered in a throaty voice. "I just wanted to feel how smooth your skin was."

Minutes passed by before D-money started kissing her on the neck. Kissing on the neck felt good and it was a safe zone for her, she thought. Trying to watch the movie, the kissing intensified. Then he started squeezing her inner thigh.

Heat transformed into heavy breathing; her breath caught in her throat. Janiece turned her face toward his lips and started kissing him back. Passionate, hot-wet kisses ignited between them. He pressed the back of her head with his left hand as he explored her tongue, deeply.

He grabbed her size A cup breast and squeezed them roughly. He took the initiative and placed her right hand on his crotch. She felt the hardening pole strain against the seat of his pants.

Caught up in the mix, Janiece forgot that she was a virgin. She pictured losing her virginity to someone she loved not just met. When she bounced back to reality, she found herself stretch on her back and D-money on top of her, his breathing hot on her neck.

"No," she whined.

"Shhh," he muttered against her neck.

"Wait…wait…Noooo," she shrieked. "Get off me."

He desired her but she wasn't ready. She felt her body sinking further down in his bed by his weight. He fumbled with her shorts. His lips suckled harder on her neck. It was tiresome as she struggled underneath, twisting and turning. She glanced to the side. Her eyes landed on his Lil' Kim poster. She gazed down and felt around for his hand. She brought it up to her mouth and bit his fingers.

He instantly froze, yelling. "Ouch bitch! What the

hell?" he said eyeing her.

Janiece pushed back, sat up and rolled off the bed, pushing her shirt down. "You was gon' to rape me?"

Rape. "You wanted it as much as I did so don't try to play. You ain't gonna say that I tried to rape you?"

"Not if you let me leave right now."

Filled with anger, he hollered. "Get your shit and get out of my house!"

Janiece quickly stepped around to slip in her sandals and grabbed her purse while watching D-money. She took off like Flo Jo running to the apartments. Out of breath and hair disarrayed, Janiece stepped through the door. Mya was lying on the sofa watching TV.

"I told you to take that condom with you. How did it feel?" she asked with a smirk.

Chapter 7

How long will you who are simple love your simple ways... Proverbs 1:22.

Janiece

It had been two days since Janiece left the bedroom. The only time the door was opened was when she went to the bathroom or to grab something to eat. Today was the fourth of July which meant she knew Mya and she was going to go to the club. She never told Mya about D-money. To her, it was a figment of her imagination like it never happened.

Mya knocked on her door and she opened it. Mya held two cups in her hand. "Here," Mya pushed one cup in her hand. She could tell that Mya had been drinking before now because of her loud smelling breath.

"Get ready for the club. It's the fourth of July so you know we got to go dancing."

And then Mya turned and left her standing there with the cup in her hand. Janiece stepped back into the room with the half cup of Grey Goose. She put the cup up to her lips and swallowed. She gasped because it burned the inside of her lungs badly. She let out a shrieking noise, "Ahhhhh!" When she drunk the rest of the Grey Goose, she cried for her mama and for her grandparents and then cracked a smile when she thought about her grandparents. And then the tears rushed out of her eyes. Life was good once. Why me? She cried as she allowed the burning sensation to hit the back of her throat.

Club Train was located in the bottom part of LaGrange. That's where most of the low income and drug dealers lived. This club was for those twenty-one years old and older. Mya's boyfriend knew the manager of the club so they could get in for free. Mya gripped her arm and side-stepped some men.

"Excuse us," Mya shouted as they strutted passed them.

Janiece's eyes widened when she saw women dancing on poles. Some women were dancing inside of cages on the stage. It had a large dance floor as well. The club was mature with an exotic theme. Even the waitresses had a uniform. They were dressed in a maid outfit but with more ass cheeks exposed.

Still holding onto her arm, Mya led her to a table that was already occupied by two men. As soon as Mya walked up behind one guy, she kissed him on the neck. He turned around and it was Derrell.

He smiled, "Sup Janiece."

"Hey."

He turned toward the guy sitting at the table. "This my boy Ritz."

"Huh?"

"I'm Ritz!" he hollered.

She looked over at the one hundred and fifty pound, dark brown haired, and green-eyed man looking up to her. He was attractive for a white guy.

"Oh, nice to meet you," she stated as she grabbed a chair and sat down next to him.

"Likewise," he said and averted his attention to the woman sliding down the pole in a bikini.

Janiece's song Clumsy by Fergie blared through the speakers. Mya had left her with Ritz while she and

Derrell disappeared in the club somewhere. Bouncing her head and singing along to the lyrics, she observed Ritz's pulsating muscles under his Michael Vick jersey.

A cinnamon-colored complexion woman with red extensions stopped and whispered something in Ritz's ear. As she spoke to him, he grabbed her butt cheek. Janiece observed all that transpired in front of her.

White Girl by Young Jeezy played next.

Still sexually holding her, the woman said something because Ritz turned around and cracked a smile at her. Being polite, she smiled back. The woman left and Ritz scooted closer to her and struck up a conversation.

"How come you ain't shakin' that ass on the floor?"

"Don't know," she shrugged her shoulders.

"I know what will get you on the dance floor," he said as he flagged another waitress down.

A cute Hispanic woman walked toward the table and stopped in front of him. "What can I get you guys?" she asked, beaming at Ritz.

He looked over to Janiece. "What're you drinkin' on?"

Janiece shrugged her shoulders again and told Ritz to bring her anything.

"What can I get you, Ritz?" the waitress asked, keeping her eyes trained on him the entire time.

"Bring me a Heineken and a Long Island Iced Tea," he stated, his voice businesslike.

She glared at him when he took out a fifty-dollar bill and told the waitress to keep the change. The waitress smiled gratefully and sashayed away with their order.

Since it was her first-time meeting Ritz, she figured he had the money the way he tipped the waitress. She smiled inwardly as she inspected him from a distance. Ritz didn't show his wealth by flaunting it gregariously. He donned a gold chain necklace and a gold watch iced out in diamonds. She considered him to be low-key compared to Derrell. Derrell had two diamond stud earrings, a platinum necklace, bracelet and a platinum ring on his pinky finger.

Minutes later, the same Hispanic waitress set the Heineken in front of Ritz. He nodded his head toward her. The waitress placed the Long Island Iced Tea in front of her. Before leaving the table, the server squatted down in front of Ritz.

"Thank you," Janiece replied as she was awestruck at the sight before her.

The woman waited patiently until Ritz leaned forward and kissed her on the forehead. The woman sprang to her feet and sauntered away. He looked over at her. "So cutie, you like your drink?" he smiled showing his pearly whites.

With eyes stretched wide, she lied. "Yeah, I have them all the time."

The drink was potent for her taste but she didn't let Ritz know. She drank it with ease. She was in a zone as she bobbed her head along with the fast tempo of a rap song. Sooner than later her head began throbbing. She was wasted as she agreed to another Long Island Iced Tea. The pounding in her head boomed thunderously. The room was spinning. She felt nauseous. With a slurred speech, she asked. "Where's Mya?"

"She left with Derrell."

"Oh," was all she said.

"You ready to go?"

"Yeah," she muttered.

She really didn't remember when or how she made it to Mya's apartment but Ritz was asking her where her keys were.

"Janiece," he called. "You home. You gotta key?"

Janiece groaned. He then exited his side and walked around to her side. He opened the door and pulled her out. He then picked her up and carried her up the flight of stairs. Putting her on the ground, he asked, "You got your key?"

Janiece mumbled, "I'm drunk. Pocket."

"What?" he asked in a calm tone.

"Pocket."

"Okay," he said as he fished for the key in her left pocket first and that's where he found it. He inserted the key and opened the door as he guided Janiece behind him as he shut the door. "Where's your room?"

"To the left."

She felt herself being tugged by someone and then the person opened her door to the room. She felt safe somehow. The person told her to get in the bed but before she could she asked. "What time is it?"

"It's three in the morning," a man's voice said. "I'll lock the door behind me on the way out."

"Ritz?"

"Yeah it's me," was all she remembered before closing her eyes to sleep.

Chapter 8

Whose ways are crooked, and they forward in their paths...Proverbs 2:15.

Ritz

"Sup, you always get drunk when you're out with Mya?" Ritz asked as he entered Derrell's apartment.

Janiece cut her eyes at him with a shocked expression. "How'd you get in here? I know I locked the doors when Mya left."

"Chill!" he said, "Derrell gave me the key while he and Mya are downstairs. So what was up with you last week?"

"Um, I was wasted. I usually don't get that drunk when I'm out."

"So you good?" he asked intrigued.

"Yeah, so what prompted you to come to see me today?"

His throat made a chortled sound. His green eyes darkened as he ogled her. For him to pick a woman and train her, she had to have something exotic about herself.

And it was something remarkable about her appearance. She had a splatter of freckles spilled across the bridge of her nose and cheeks. With her fair skin and light yellow-brown undertone and long brown hair, she was that and more. She was a dime piece in his book. Ritz saw the innocence within her. Ritz knew he could control her mind easily. He had women at his beck and call so Janiece would be easy to pull. He knew she wasn't sexually active. And he was fine with that. He didn't want to be her first either. He had other plans for her.

He ignored her question but instead asked his own. "So, you got a man?"

"Do you have a girlfriend?"

He arched his eyebrows because he was caught off guard. Being the player that he was, he answered, "Nah those girls are nothing but hoes but if you play your cards right you'll be my main girl."

"What makes you think that you stand a chance?" she asked playfully.

"I was just sayin'."

"Sayin' what?" she questioned him.

In the past, he slapped a bitch for questioning him but since he was trying to hook her, he played her little game. She intrigued him. It brought out her personality. "If you were my girl then you would be getting a weekly allowance. That's only if you were my main girl."

He could tell that she was thinking of his question. "So I heard that you like to shop?" he reached into his back pocket and took out his wallet. He pulled a bunch of twenties and flashed them in front of her face. Her eyes lit up. Money was the key. His lips curved into a cunning smile. "I'm gon' to ask this one more time. Do you have a man?"

"No," she muttered. "How old are you?"

"Twenty-five. That's gon' to be a problem?"

"No, it's cool. So how do I know that I can trust you?"

"If I didn't take advantage of you when you were sloppy drunk on the fourth then I'm trustworthy in your eyes, right?"

"Yeah, good point. I was out of it. I didn't get out of bed 'til two the next day."

"Uh-huh," was all he said. "So what were you watchin' on TV before I scared you?" he asked, sliding down on the sofa next to her.

"Uh, just music videos on BET," she handed him the remote. "You can change it if you wanna."

"Nah, I'm good," he said as he put his arms around his head. His phone beeped. He pulled out his cellphone and checked it. He faced Janiece. "Being my girl is a privilege. I'mma show you what it takes. In the end, you will be rewarded."

Since he didn't hear her reject him, he pulled out a blunt and a lighter. He lit it and puffed. He passed it to her.

She shook her head.

"You're scared to get a little smoke in your lungs," Ritz stated as he laughed.

"No, I just don't smoke," she stated.

"That's that high school shit," he said then cut his eyes. "Oh my bad, you are."

"I was but that's another story."

"Is that so? You care to talk about it?"

She turned her head side to side.

"Well shit," he passed her the blunt again. When she faced him, he burst out laughing.

"What's funny?"

"Some shit I was thinkin' about."

"What?" she asked out of curiosity.

Ritz stopped laughing and looked at her.

"What?" she asked.

"Nothin'. You wanna smoke?" he maneuvered the blunt toward Janiece's face.

Third time.

"If you my girl then you gotta smoke too."

"Your girl? I didn't know we established that."

"Fuck yeah. You want to spend my money, Lil ma'," he chuckled. "Now slide your fine ass ova here." On cue, she slid closer to him. He puffed and exhale the smoke.

Without Ritz saying another word, Janiece snatched the blunt out of his hand. "Shit, you almost dropped my shit!"

"I'm sorry."

"Do you know how to smoke it?" he asked in a daze.

"No."

"Hold it at the end. When you put it in your mouth, inhale slowly and exhale after you puff."

He watched her as she inhaled too much smoke. She started coughing heavily, choking on weed. He patted her on the back as she patted herself on her chest.

"Good try but you did it too fast. You got to slow your roll."

After repeatedly grasping the concept of smoking a blunt, Janiece was soon hooked. Later on that night, they had a party with weed and alcohol which was the highlight of the night. That continued almost another week before Ritz had her eating out of the palms of his hands.

Chapter 9

*When you follow the desires of your sinful nature, the results are...idolatry, drunkenness, wild parties...
Galatians 5: 19-21.*

Janiece

Strolling through LaGrange Mall on Ritz's arm, wearing daisy dukes and a blue tank top, Janiece proudly walked like she was God's gift on earth to men. She walked with confidence with her head held high because she scored a baller who had money. Couldn't nobody tell her nothing now? She walked in heels switching her hips like they were going to break. As she passed by Bath and Body Works, Janiece quickly walked toward the shoe store Bombay pulling Ritz into the store with her. She realized she could really trust him when he showered her with gifts and money. He hadn't tried anything with her sexually. She guessed Mya was right. She could have anything her heart desired if she played her cards right.

"Calm down, there ain't no need to rush," Ritz said after she let go of his arm and gravitated toward the shoes that were displayed on the front rack of the store.

"Ooh these are cute," she uttered, picking up a black and gold pump with a three-inch heel.

She eyed him out her peripheral view walked back out the store and sat on the bench in front of the store. She saw him pull out his iPhone. Whomever he was talking too it wasn't any of her business. As Mya would state, what they do is what they do as long as he balling, she remembered. It appeared as if he was agitated with the other person because she heard him say a few curses. Just then she walked out of the store and stood in front of him while he chatted away. Whoever he was talking too, he was speaking so low on the phone.

"Hold on for a sec," Ritz said to his phone. "What's up?"

"Can I get some shoes?"

"Sure just let me know when you're finished," he said as he shooed her away.

Janiece walked down three aisles of shoes before reaching for a pair of red pumps. She walked out of the store and waved to Ritz.

"I found 'em," she whispered, holding the shoes in the air.

He only smiled and shooed his hand toward her. In her mind, it meant to grab another pair and she did. Janiece happily skipped back inside the store to grab the pumps and pick up a pair of size eight blue patent leather pumps. She started walking toward the edge of the store when she saw Ritz walk into the store after ending the call. Ritz waved his hands toward the cashier. The cashier totaled the price of the shoes. While Ritz pulled out his wallet and paid for the shoes, Janiece stood on the side of him. Ritz pulled out a hundred-dollar bill and gave it to the cashier. The cashier then gave Ritz fifty-nine dollars and sixty-three cents and put the boxes in a Bombay bag. Janiece grabbed the bag as they walked out of the store.

As they exited the mall, Ritz threw his keys at her. "You wanna drive?"

"Yeah but I don't have my driver's license though."

"No problem just don't drive fast," he quickly said, "You do know how to drive, don't you?"

"Yeah, I used to drive my Grandpa around the

neighborhood."

Unlocking the doors to his '11 Cadillac Escalade, Janiece hopped in the driver's seat. She remembered what her Grandpa used to say before pulling off in a car. 'Always make sure your seat is well adjusted.' Looking around for the seat adjustment buttons, she finally found them just in time Ritz told her where they were located.

"The seat adjustments are on the left side of the seat."

Feeling dumb, Janiece yelled, "Yeah, I know I was just messing' wit you!"

"Sure." Ritz cranked up some Hip-Hop music as he puffed on a cigarillo, full of weed that was lying in the ashtray.

Her song Falsetto by Dream boomed through the speakers as she began to sing. She was in her own world. In her peripheral view, she saw Ritz looking at her but she kept on singing. She let her window down to let out some of the smoke. She was told once by her grandpa that she had a beautiful voice. Suddenly her heart felt heavy thinking of her grandpa.

"You can blow Mami," he said as he replaced his

cigarillo in the ashtray.

Blushing, Janiece quit singing.

"Nah, don't stop singin' ma'. I was givin' you a compliment. Derrell know you can sing?" he asked in a sly tone.

"Nah, Mya don't know either."

"What? You can make a lot of money shawty. So you like to sing in the shower and stuff?"

"Yeah pretty much," she responded as she concentrated on the road. She wondered what Ritz was thinking since he found out she can sing.

He picked up his cigarillo and shouted, "Sing that shit!"

Pulling up to the apartments, Janiece cut off the car, grabbed her bags, and stepped out the car with Ritz. She hit the lock button on the keychain. Then they walked up the stairs to the second floor of the apartment. She inserted her house key but she realized it was already unlocked. She twisted the doorknob and pushed open the door to find Derrell and Mya in the heat of the moment.

"Oh shit, I forgot to lock the door," she heard Derrell

say.

Mya jumped up, covering her breasts with her hands, and ran toward their bedroom. Derrell taking his time, got up, dapped Ritz's hand, looked at her with a mischievous smile and then left the living room. Janiece locked the door behind them and then walked to her room to put her shoes in the room when she heard Mya moaning. Janiece shook her head and placed her shoes by the dresser. When she walked back into the living room, Ritz had lit a cigarillo. She sat on one end while he smoked his weed. He offered it to her and she grabbed it. She only smoked if he offered it to her.

Chapter 10

The Lord helps the fallen and lifts those bent beneath their loads. Psalm 145:14.

Janiece

A month later

Janiece was standing on the corner wearing short shorts, black heels, hoop earrings, and a low-cut top on Pearson and Eighth Street. It was ten o'clock on a Friday night. She had been waiting on the corner for thirty minutes waiting for 'the ride.' Feet hurting, people walking by, and men whistling, Janiece finally gave up and sat on the edge of the sidewalk. Not a minute later, a dark, tinted window of a black Cadillac Seville STS rolled up. Janiece quickly stood up and walked toward the vehicle.

The passenger rolled down the window and spoke in a low voice, "Pin-pin green machine."

Janiece sashayed to the building behind her and lifted up a cardboard box that revealed a medium-size black bag. She picked it up and presented it to the passenger.

He then reached down and gave Janiece a flower bag in exchange.

"You do extras?" he asked in a slick voice.

"No," was all she said and left.

Janiece walked a few miles before spotting Ritz's Escalade on the corner of Fourth and Fifth Street.

"You got it?" he asked.

"Yeah," she said as she gave him the bag before walking around to get in the SUV.

He hurriedly unzipped the bag and saw its contents. He grinned widely.

"What's in it?" Janiece asked.

Without looking at her, he said, "Nothing. It's not for you to know but just do."

Feeling hurt by his remarks, she quietly asked, "How'd I do?"

This time turning toward her, he said, "You did a good job. I guess you know what that means."

"What?" she asked in a dumbfounded tone.

"You get paid Mami," he paused. "You want to go shoppin' tomorrow or you want me to take you out to eat?"

"Shoppin'," she said hastily.

"Well I'll pick you up tomorrow at six so be ready," he said as he drove her back to Mya's apartment.

Exactly at six pm, Ritz was outside waiting for Janiece to jump in his ride to take her shopping for her hard work. They went to Macy's, JCPenney's, Dillard's, and some other stores. That day they both walked out with six bags full of clothes, jewelry, and shoes. Their first business venture was successful and they both enjoyed the fruits of their labor in LaGrange Mall.

The next night Janiece wore a burgundy wig with blue heels, a blue top, and black shorts exposing her long, yellow legs on Little and Big Street at midnight. Two cars pulled over and asked Janiece for some fun but she gave them some unkindly remarks and refused their offer no matter how much they suggested.

Then suddenly a four-door red Honda pulled up to the curve. A tall, muscular black man and a lanky white guy exited the car and stepped onto the sidewalk. She faced them, backing up and trying not to make eye contact with them.

"Hey ma'am, me and my partner were wonderin'—"

Partner, did he say? Janiece thought. Oh shit, they think I'm a prostitute.

"I'm sorry but what did you say?"

"I said what're you offering'?" asked the man as he stepped closer in her direction.

"Nothing. I'm not what you think I am."

He glowered in her direction. "What the fuck are you?"

"A businesswoman!" she shouted.

"A businesswoman, huh? What type of business do you run?"

"None of your business," she answered in a shaky voice. She just knew she was doing Ritz some favors as he put it. Janiece tried to walk away when the guy persisted that he and his friend wanted some pussy. She turned and looked him squarely in the eyes.

"Wait...just talk to me," the man's voice vibrated nearby.

Janiece panicked. Her heart began pounding. These

men were trying to get her. She forgot about the bag. Began to retrace her steps. Her heels click-clacked along the sidewalk.

"Johnny, call-in number thirty-four. We got ourselves a prostitute on the prowl."

Oh shit, they're cops! She paused briefly, balancing on one foot at a time to snatch the heels off. She instantly picked up speed and hauled ass into a dark alley. Hid behind a big trash can. She heard sirens then saw blue lights flashing. "Oh my God!" she whispered and quivered underneath the humid weather.

After the coast was clear, she was too shaken up to go back to Mya's apartment. Knowing Mya, she would probably laugh in her face so the only place she felt comfortable was at Jennifer's. Janiece sprinted four blocks from one side of town to the other while holding her heels in her hand. Knocking on the door persistently, someone opened it. It was one of her brothers.

"Is Jennifer home?"

The boy shook his head yes and opened the door wider for Janiece to step through. "You can sit down. I'll go get her."

"Ay Jennifer, you have some messed up girl out there," she heard the little boy say.

Jennifer quickly appeared in the living room. "What happened? Why you shakin'? Let's go to my room."

Janiece followed Jennifer into her room. She threw her shoes on the floor and sat next to Jennifer on the edge of her bed. She looked around her room. She owned posters of Selena, Missy Elliot, and Usher on her wall. Her friend had a daybed. It was cozy. She recalled when she had a room such as this. Out of nowhere, the tears came pouring out of her eyes.

"Ssh, whatever happens, don't worry about it." Jennifer wrapped her arms around her and it felt so good for someone to care about her. "It's gon' to be alright."

Janiece attempted to speak but no words formed.

"Wait right here, I'm gonna grab you something to drink and you can tell me what happened tonight," Jennifer said as she dashed out the room. Seconds later, she returned with a cup of Kool-Aid. She wiped her tears away with the back of her hand.

Still shaking, Janiece opened her mouth. "I-I was almost arrested tonight."

"For what," Jennifer exclaimed then remembered to shut her bedroom because of her nosey little brothers. Her mama was working tonight.

"I do a lil' business on the side for a friend and while I was doing it. I was approached by a man and he kept askin' me questions and then I took off and then I heard the sirens."

"So he was undercover?" asked Jennifer peering at her.

"Yeah, I guess so," Janiece stated as she put the Kool-Aid to her lips.

"Where was your friend?"

"At home, I guess," replied Janiece.

"You don't know? You did that by yourself?" Jennifer asked as she sat down on her bed glaring at Janiece.

She nodded her head.

"I wouldn't have guessed that you strip. You don't seem like the type."

"I don't!" Janiece snapped.

Jennifer held her arms in the air. "My bad then what do you do?"

"Business."

"How can I help you if you don't start from the beginning? Tell me what's up?"

Janiece revealed that she worked for a guy named Ritz. As she was telling Jennifer pieces of information, she scrutinized Jennifer's sneering expressions.

"Lately he has me to stand on the corner to swap some bags with his business associates."

"Hold up, you're gonna tell me that you're not prostituting yourself but you're selling drugs for this man? Are you crazy? Do you know you can go to jail and I won't be able to chill with you no more?"

"It's not drugs," Janiece adamantly replied.

"How do you know? Have you asked him?"

"No," she said shamefully.

"Is he getting something in return?"

"No!"

Jennifer eyed her. "Are you sure? You don't have to

say what you do for him but are you don' it?"

"I told you no. All that I get out of it is to go shopping."

"You do his dirty work and he takes you to go shopping? That is some messed up shit. He's like your pimp. Why are you messing' with him like that? If you don't know it by now he's bad business!" Jennifer exclaimed vehemently in a forceful tone. "You know he's gon' to want something in return. Why would Ritz do that for nothing? Believe it or not, but he's going to ask for it."

"Nah, I don't believe it. He's too nice and plus we've been seeing each other for two months now."

"Yeah whatever, I know men. Some of them are triflin'." Jennifer touched her hand softly and spoke, "You need to get a cell phone before something crazy happens."

"I plan to soon as I save up enough money but thanks for hearing me out. I should be getting back home. I know Mya is probably lookin' for me."

"You're welcome. Let me walk you out."

Janiece peeped over her shoulder at Jennifer and shook her head. She couldn't understand that she didn't have anyone to help her. To save her. She believed in her heart that she was alone in this world. With Ritz on her side, she had good benefits. She hugged and thanked Jennifer for her hospitality as she walked the long-stretch home to Mya's apartment.

Chapter 11

Those who are dominated by the sinful nature think
about sinful things...Romans 8:5-7.

Janiece

As soon as Janiece stepped inside the apartment, she
was scolded for leaving the bag at the scene of the
incident. "Where you been girl? Do you know Ritz has
been lookin' for you the past hour?" Mya exclaimed.

An hour? It had been three hours since her ordeal
went down and he just started looking for her. Maybe
Jennifer was right. "Where is he now?"

"Still out. Maybe you need to call him and let him
know that you're here."

Janiece strolled over to the sofa, picked up the
cordless phone, and walked in the backroom. She dialed
his cell. He answered on the fifth ring. He must not have
been worrying about her too hard because he didn't
answer on the first ring.

"Where the fuck are you!"

He wasn't worried about her wellbeing and it

saddened her, "At Mya's."

"You got the stuff?"

She was afraid to answer him. "No, cops were after me but the bag is still at the corner where I left it under a wooden crate."

"You checked it to see if it was still there or are you basin' it on assumptions?"

Nervously, she answered, "Assumptions."

Click.

No how are you don' or are you alright? For the next few days, Janiece didn't hear from Ritz.

Monday evening

Wanting to enjoy her Monday evening because no one was here. She flipped through the television and began watching a music video. Twenty minutes later, her happiness went out the door when the apartment door opened and Ritz breezed through the door running his hands through his hair. Her eyes got real big.

Ritz laughed. "Sup shawty, you good?"

"Yeah. Where Mya and Derrell?" she asked, looking toward the closed door. Her heart began to beat rapidly.

She wasn't afraid of Ritz but she didn't know for sure. She watched him as he sat on the sofa beside her.

"Derrell down the street and gave me his key," he faced her. "Are you wonderin' if I'm still mad at you? The answer is no. I was just pissed," he reached over and pulled her closer to him.

Snuggled tightly under him, she mumbled, "Pissed at me for leaving your bag or me being almost caught?"

Ritz kissed her on the forehead and hugged her. "Nah mami, I was pissed at those cops. I'm glad my bag was still where you left it because I would have been in trouble if somebody else scooped up my stock."

"I'm sorry but I was scared though. I just know that something told me to run and I did."

"No prob mami. I would have done the same thing."

During Lil Wayne's video Takeover on Fuse, Janiece tilted her head up toward Ritz's face.

"What're you lookin' at?"

"You," was all she replied.

"For what?" asked Ritz.

"Just thinkin' about what you actually do for a

113

livin'?"

This time he stopped looking at the video and faced her. "What you mean?" he asked her nonchalantly.

"Like your business."

"What about it? Why are you so interested in what I do now? Who you been talkin' to?"

"Nobody," she spat, shaking her head.

"Nobody has you askin' me questions you don't suppose to be askin' me," he looked at her sideways.

"I mean I was almost caught and I thought like...I mean if I'm doin' you favors...like what am I?"

He chuckled and answered, "You're a messenger."

"A messenger? What kind of messenger?" she asked with a smirk.

"A foot messenger."

She sat up straighter on the sofa. "What's a foot messenger?"

"Someone who delivers packages."

"Then what are you?"

"I'm a carrier," he stated, his voice rough.

She waited a few moments before asking the

inevitable question. "Are those drugs that I carry around in your bag?"

"Awe shit, I missed a part of the video," he said trying to dismiss her question. "See you're askin' too many questions. You got to be quiet."

She sat quietly for a few minutes but thought of Jennifer. "Are those drugs, Ritz? I just want to know that's all."

He looked at her and said, "I know what you need."

She watched him pull out a blunt and a lighter. He lit it, puffed, and passed it to her.

He did that hoping it would shut her up but it didn't. She was curious and had to know where she stood with Ritz. "If I get caught for carrying drugs, would I get locked up for a while?"

"Don't worry about it."

"But what if I did?" she asked, nervously as she puffed on the blunt.

"I'll get you out. I'm your man, right?"

She nodded her head.

"Then you don't need to worry about anything else.

Just smoke and relax. I know you're still shakin' up from what happened to you Saturday night. I'm sorry that I didn't ask how you were don' then, I was scared myself. I don't want you to worry though, okay?"

"Okay," she replied.

They finished watching the music video when suddenly the door flew open. Derrell walked inside of the apartment with people trailing behind him.

"Guess who I found," Derrell stated as he waited inside of his kitchen. "Anna."

Chapter 12

A scoundrel plots evil and his speech is like a scorching fire. Proverbs 16:27

Janiece

Anna? Who the hell is this Anna? Janiece thought. She felt the atmosphere change between her and Ritz. Just then four women walked inside the apartment. They were all attractive. A petite Asian woman with long black hair with thick thighs. A butterscotch toned woman with a voluptuous butt, an olive tanned beauty with big breast, and a curvy built, toffee brown woman with a reddish undertone and big lips.

"What have y'all been up to?" Derrell asked in a jovial tone.

"Shit chillin'. What's poppin' tonight?" asked Ritz.

"A lil' drinking and card playin'."

"That's what's up."

Ritz sprang to his feet and strolled toward the kitchen table. He sat down with a group of guys. Two of the women sat on the sofa with their backs turned toward her.

The hell? Y'all can get up and leave for all I care, Janiece mused.

The Asian woman stared at her with a scowl and pulled a chair and sat down closer to her friends. The big breasted woman pulled a chair and sat next to her.

Smoke filled the atmosphere, women, and men laughing, TV playing, and music booming while Janiece sat on the sofa feeling invisible. Every now and then, she would glance at Ritz as he sat with a beer in one hand and poker chips in the other. The women talked within the circle. As they were talking, the Asian woman would occasionally look toward her and laugh.

What the hell you laughing at? Janiece pondered as she sent a fake smile back at her guest.

Laughter and high fiving each other, she heard Ritz holler at no one in particular. "Light me a blunt!" She witnessed as the Asian woman stood up on cue. She was frozen in place. She ain't never had to do this but this woman got under her skin for some reason. She didn't know what she had to prove but she better sit down somewhere for all she cared. She guarded as the woman walking over to Ritz, sliding her right hand into her back pocket, leaning over, and lighting his blunt while looking back at her with a sneer. Janiece scanned the room and noticed the other women were whispering to each other and giggling.

Janiece had enough when the big breasted woman, spoke to her. "Hi, I'm Kelley and you're?"

"Janiece."

"Nice to meet you."

"Same here," Janiece smiled coyly.

"Do you know who we are?" Kelley asked.

"No," Janiece answered nonchalantly.

"Well," she said. "We're the 'IT' girls. Anything goes we do. So are you a newcomer?"

"' IT' girls? You mean to tell me y'all do anything that they say?"

"Yeah. You too right?"

"No!"

"Then what do you do?" she asked persistently.

"I don't do anything. I'm Ritz girl."

After she said that, Kelley laughed in her face. She

stared as Kelley walked over to the Asian woman and whispered something in her ear. The woman turned and slowly made her way toward her and bent close to her face.

"You're nothing but another girl to Ritz. Do you actually think you're his only girl?"

"No, I didn't say I was," she explained. "But I am his girl and who are you to be up in my face?"

"Bitch, I'll tell you. I'm his main woman Anna. If you have a problem with that I suggest you take it up with Ritz. But ain't no need to do that. He knows where home is," she said in a whisper not wanting to distract the men from gambling.

"Calm down, that ain't nothing but a child," Shontae suggested, the toffee-brown skinned woman with the big lips.

"Well she needs to take her ass home," Anna replied.

"Bitch," Janiece retorted. "You take your ass home." She didn't even know that type of language was in her until tonight.

"Whoa, take it easy ladies!" someone yelled from the

poker table.

"No, this child needs to go home," Anna said with anger, pointing her fingers toward Janiece.

"Aye dawg, you got two women fightin' over you."

"Come here Anna," Ritz responded.

Janiece looked at Ritz like he had lost his mind. Just a minute ago, he had said he cared about her and now he takes this woman side over hers. Janiece blew out a loud sigh. She glared as Anna planted a kiss on Ritz's lips. Janiece felt flushed. She felt the heat burning on her ears. She had never been jealous of no female, not even Mya but this Anna rubbed her the wrong way. She squinted her eyes as Anna strutted like she was on a runway show across the room, rolling her eyes at her.

Janiece rolled her eyes back. She cocked her neck to the side and glowered at Anna. It was as if someone snapped their fingers because the 'IT' girls were servicing the men. Janiece watched in awe as the women lit blunts, poured drinks, and laughed at corny jokes. It was well past one in the morning that the party was still going. She hoped wherever Mya was that she was alright.

Suddenly Ritz had got up from the table and strolled down the hallway toward the bathroom. She stared as Anna walked behind him like a dog. As her eyes followed Anna, she heard whispers from the other women.

She faced them. "Can I help y'all?"

The women shook their heads. Something caught her eyes. Janiece stared down the hallway and Anna was propped up against the door. Janiece sighed out loud. She watched the women turned to stare at her while she scrutinized Anna's sleazy moves. Janiece learned early on thanks to Jennifer's lesson that she had to portray that she was just as crazy as the women in her circle. Inside her mind, she cursed Anna out a thousand times already. *Stupid bitch! The fuck! Ritz can't pee in peace.*

Chapter 13

Do not speak in the hearing of a fool, for he will
despise the wisdom of your words. Proverbs 23:9.

Janiece

The door creaked.

"Sup with you," she heard the woman ask *her* Ritz in a cat-like, seductive tone.

"Nothin', what's good ma?"

Janiece folded her arms across her chest and gave them an evil stare.

"You," the woman answered him.

She noticed how Ritz tried to avoid Anna but she caught hold of his shirt. Anna faced her with a cunning smirk on her face before pulling Ritz's neck down and devouring his mouth with sloppy kisses. As Anna kissed him, she tugged on his shirt and stood in front of him, glancing back at her. She then started pushing Ritz toward her room. As soon as Janiece read Anna's mind, she attempted to intervene briskly marching down the hall but it was too late when her bedroom door was slammed shut in her face.

Janiece knocked and banged on the door repeatedly. The other women came down the hall and told Janiece to give it up because they were about to fuck.

"Uh not in my bed."

Kelley shook her head and said, "You can forget about it. Anna is don' business." They walked off while Janiece stayed there beating on the door.

She heard loud moaning coming from Anna and a bitch scream come from Ritz. She figured he was getting his dick sucked. "That's foul, you stupid ass bitch!" Janiece retorted, beating on the door once before walking away.

She stomped down the hallway and glanced over to Derrell's smug face. She flopped down on the sofa. She crossed her arms over her chest. She hoped someone said something to her so she could go off on them. But no one dared. Soon the door opened and she heard their voices of laughter as they joined them in the living room. Her eyes were trained on Ritz's appearance.

He glared back and kept on walking until someone

told him to check his fly. When he looked down, he zipped up and sat at the poker table to resume his game.

She knew better than to say anything to Ritz. She didn't blame him. The hatred in her eyes burned for Anna as the 5'2 she-devil in patent leather pants sat across from her on the far end of the room, mean-mugging her.

It was much later when Janiece sauntered inside her room to air it out. The foul stench of sex hit her hard in the nose and she gagged. Turned red in the face. She snatched the blankets from the bedding and threw them in the washing machine. She opened the window and walked into the bathroom to retrieve the air freshener. She sprayed until it caught inside of her lungs. She coughed and left the room. Janiece walked over to the closet, yanked open the curtains and laid some sheets onto the bed. She couldn't focus right. Her mind wandered to a faraway place. She lay on top of the covers and went to sleep.

When Janiece awakened the next morning, she met Mya coming out of her room.

"Hey, where you been?" she asked in a concerned

voice.

Mya gaped at her and rolled her eyes, walking up the hallway. "I'm tired of this shit."

"Tired of what?" asked Janiece, following behind her. "Why didn't you come home last night?"

She waited for Mya to answer her but she didn't. She followed suit inside the kitchen to grab a bowl of Fruit Loops.

"Shit, he has me workin' too hard," Mya mumbled before putting a spoonful of cereal in her mouth as she sat down in the kitchen.

Janiece sat opposite her in the chair.

"I gotta find me another way to make money," Mya turned toward Janiece. "When are you gon' to get a job again? I need-I mean we need some money."

"Ugh, I guess sometime soon."

"Well you need to hurry up or something," she said pausing, "Janiece, Ritz ain't never try nothing with you?"

Janiece shook her head. "Just kissing on the forehead and smoking blunts but nah."

"Shit, why I gotta do stuff?"

"Do what?" Janiece inquired.

"This is grown shit. Don't be worryin' about me. You betta be lucky that you're still a virgin."

"Okay, but why did you say that you were tired of don' stuff?"

Mya snapped, "Stay out of grown folks business."

"Well excuse…" Janiece said returning to her Fruit Loops.

Mya jumped up mad, tossed the bowl in the sink, and stalked to her room. When she stepped out, she was wearing a black tank top with blue shorts and black flip-flops. She snatched her keys off the wooden crate.

"Where you gon' dressed like that?"

"To church."

Janiece burst out laughing.

"What! I can't go to church?" Mya asked, her voice provoked.

"Not dressed like that you can't."

"You don't know a damn thing," Mya retorted and left the apartment.

"Whoa, what set her off?" Janiece asked herself,

leisurely walking toward the remote on the wooden crate. She flipped through the channels finally landing on MTV.

Watching music videos started taking a toll on her sleepiness so she laid her head on the arm on the sofa and drifted off to sleep. The ringing of the cordless phone jarred her from her sleep five minutes later. She sat upright. She looked around for the phone. Grabbed the cordless phone and said, "Hello."

"Sup lil' ma. I got a new gig for you," Ritz said speaking businesslike again.

"What's the gig?"

"Since you can sing, I got a gig where you sing for some money. It's like being your own boss. You want to get paid like a boss, right? Then you already know that I get a cut of your money because I put you on the spot. So you being my lil' ma, I expect some payback."

She nodded her head knowing Ritz couldn't see her. She listened but figured with these two gigs she could set money aside and save some herself. Since Mya didn't know how much she was bringing in then she wouldn't know how much she was keeping for herself. Mya was a money-hungry person, to her.

Every other night she would alternate between a foot messenger and singing inside a club to earn a few dollars.

In the wee hours of Monday morning around two, Janiece walked into her room and yelled, "What the hell!" she glared around the room and her clothes were piled on top of her bed. Her first thought was Mya. What was Mya looking for? Exhausted after walking and standing around being a foot messenger, she collapsed on top of clothes.

Boom. Boom.

Her body jerked to the thunderous sound. She opened her eyes and stared up at the ceiling.

Boom. Boom.

The sound came again. The doorknob rattled. She faced the door and realize the knob was jiggling. *When did she lock her door?* She didn't remember locking the door but maybe she did. She was tired after coming in after two in the morning.

"Janiece, get up and unlock the door! I know you up!" Mya shouted. "Open the damn door!" Mya yelled repeatedly, hitting the door.

Janiece scrambled out of bed and staggered toward the door. She unlocked the door and Mya barged in, turning the light on and pushing her out the way.

How rude! Janiece cringed under the bright lights.

"I need to borrow a hundred dollars now since you makin' money."

"One hundred dollars? That's a lot. I got fifty," exclaimed Janiece.

"Then give me that. Derrell is havin' another poker night on Wednesday. I gotta buy some cleaning supplies. I want the fifty dollars no later than today. I know you got the money."

"What happened to my room?" Janiece asked.

Mya tossed over her shoulders as she was leaving out the room. "Oh, I was lookin' for that red skirt I let you borrow last week."

"Yeah right," Janiece mumbled.

Chapter 14

Wherever there is jealousy and selfish ambition, there you will find disorder...James 3:16

Janiece

The party never stopped. It was only Wednesday night. *Dang, did anyone have a regular job they had to go to like normal people?* Tupac music blared through the bedroom walls from the living room. Janiece contemplated on whether she wanted to join the party or not. It had been two days since she saw Ritz after giving him his bag. She knew he would be out there. She was in her thoughts as she heard a knock at the door.

"Shit," she cussed. Just when she thought she could spend the night in her room, a knock came upon the door.

"Who is it?" she asked coyly.

"Ritz said to come out," a female voice uttered.

"Okay," she replied, her voice weak.

To her, Ritz was the coolest person to hang around with because he took care of his women. But she knew Ritz could be the meanest guy as well. Soon as someone messed up his money, the ugly side came out; just like when she left his bag and ran from the cops.

Thirty minutes later, Janiece stepped out with skin-tight jeans and a tight-fitting black shirt. There in the spotlight of the living room, folks were smoking and drinking. Mya was in her usual setting, catering to Derrell's every move and right beside him at the table was Ritz. He waved his hands for her to come to him.

"Sup lil' ma, you been hidin' from me?"

"N-nooo—" she stuttered.

"Well don't be a stranger," he said, shuffling a deck of cards in his hands. "Give me a kiss."

She ain't never had to kiss him before. She wondered what prompted that. She bent down and kissed him on the cheek and then heard laughter. She didn't know if they were laughing at her or him.

"Now is that how we do?" he asked, giving her an imminent scowl.

She swallowed the fear in her throat. She leaned down and kissed him square on the lips.

"That's more like it," he proclaimed, "Go get me a

Corona," he said and slapped her on the butt cheek.

She jumped to his order as she found herself standing beside Mya in the kitchen catering to their men.

"You finally out, huh?"

Janiece nodded her head and kept her head down. As time passed by, Ritz summoned her to sing for them. She closed her eyes and tilted her head back and sang. Song after song, Janiece had the apartment hating because of how good she sounded.

When she ended a song on a high note, she opened her eyes. Mya frowned at her. Frozen in place, she knew Mya was jealous. Mya rolled her eyes and turned on the stereo. *One More Chance* by Biggie vibrated through the thin walls. She glanced at Ritz. He twirled his hand at her to signal for her to continue and she did.

On cue, Mya began dancing and then gyrated her hips in Derrell's direction. She threw her legs up on him and rode him. Janiece figured it caused a chain reaction because all the women in the room followed suit. Janiece raised her eyebrows and gawked at them, sneaking away into the kitchen to quench her thirst. She opened the refrigerator and pulled out a coke. Soon as she shut the door, a man was right up on her and it startled her.

"Sup shawty, you can blow for real. What you do in your spare time?" he asked, his voice rough and raspy.

Annoyed by his sluggish speech, Janiece turned away from him. He grabbed her by the arm. She looked back at his yellowish, droopy eyes and unkempt dreads that fell past his shoulders. Her eyes swiftly drifted to Ritz but he was too occupied with two women grinding on him.

"Say shawty, you got a man?" the man questioned, breathing heavy.

"Yeah, I'm with Ritz."

"So is errywuovem hoes. You see you ain't no hoe, I heard. You fresh off the market."

"I *am with Ritz*," she stressed in annoyance. She wondered why this man was in her face if she already told him that she was with Ritz. Most men backed away but not this muscular guy.

"He popped that cherry yet?"

"Why you all up in my business!" she snapped. "You don't even know me like that. I suggest you get out my face before Ritz gets you for messin' with his girl."

"See, you said Ritz girl, not a woman or anything. Drop that loser and get with me. I got cheese baby."

"So does Ritz."

"But his dick ain't bigger than mine," he spoke grabbing his crotch. "I'll rip you right open. Have you screamin' my name."

She sneered at him because of his filthy language. Janiece left the kitchen and sat down on a chair by the door. The thought crossed her mind as why men considered her to be easy. Just because she engaged with their activities didn't mean she was 'fast tailed'. When the guy sat down, he began licking his lips and blowing kisses. Janiece flipped him off with her middle finger. She turned away from his disgusting behavior.

"Janiece, Janiece," Ritz called her.

She looked at him. He motioned for her to dance with the nod of his head. She shook her head because she didn't feel like entertaining these people anymore. Thinking nothing of it, she bobbed her head along to the music when suddenly a woman began walking in her direction. She froze like a deer in headlights.

The 5'5, hazel eyed, redbone, thick-ass woman stopped in front of her and held out her hand. Janiece shook her head and shooed her away. The woman faced Ritz and then back to her. The woman reached down and grabbed her hand, catching her off guard. Janiece jerked her hand away. Then the red bone woman started gyrating on her lap.

"Damn, that's hot!" a man hollered.

"That shit hot. Got me hard as hell," another man said.

It took Janiece by surprise that this woman was rotating her hips on her lap. She was embarrassed. Her face flushed. She was dumbstruck because all eyes were on her. Janiece faced Mya and pleaded for help with her eyes. Mya rolled her eyes and strutted in her direction. Mya got in between the woman and her. Suddenly Mya pushed the woman's backside forward and started gyrating her behind.

"Awe shit look at this!" someone shouted.

The attention left Janiece as all eyes were on Mya.

Janiece was thankful for that. The redbone woman and Mya were dancing with each other. Stunned by what the woman had done, Janiece got up to leave the party. Inches from her bedroom, the same man grabbed her by the waist.

"I know you liked that. That was some cool shit," he said with a smirk.

Janiece snapped, "Leave me the hell alone!"

"Oh, you just frontin'. I saw how you were teasin' me in that kitchen. You betta' watch your back..." was all he said before she shut the door in his face.

Lying down on her bed, tears flowed from her eyes. Tears, where did they come from? Did they come from missing home? Did they come from embarrassment? She didn't know but she let them fall. The party lasted until the wee hours.

Thursday afternoon, Janiece padded to the bathroom and ran into Mya coming out.

"Watch where the hell you gon'!" Mya snapped bothered.

Janiece sneered at Mya's foul mood ignoring her.

Whatever Mya was going through, she wondered why she was taking it out on her. Janiece washed her body and took care of her hygiene. When she stepped out of the bathroom, Derrell was standing next to the door. She jumped.

"Dis nigga ain't got you scared?"

"Nah, you just startled me," replied Janiece.

"Yeah. Ritz said he gonna get up with you later on today."

"Okay," she said as she headed into the bedroom for a second before walking into the living room. She glanced at Mya who was sitting on the sofa watching a TV show on BET. She marched into the kitchen to fix a bowl of cereal. Leaving the kitchen, Janiece sat on the opposite side of Mya on the sofa.

"When you gonna pay us?"

Sticking a spoonful of Trix in her mouth, Janiece answered, "Uh, I guess next Monday."

"You guess? Bitch, you need to pay us some money today. That lil' fifty dollars wasn't shit."

"Okay, I'll give you a hundred dollars. I mean I have

to pay Ritz too you know."

Mya rolled her eyes and focused on the show. Janiece didn't want to focus on Mya anymore. She had to worry about meeting with Ritz later on today.

Chapter 15

No one means all he says, and yet very few say all
they mean, for words, are slippery and thought is viscous.
Henry B. Adams.

Janiece

She met Ritz downstairs. She climbed inside his SUV
and they rode around to the other side of town. She was
in her thoughts wondering why no music was playing in
the background. She could sense something was off. She
didn't dare ask him either.

Out of the blue, Ritz asked, "What the fuck I hear
about you and Trane?"

"Trane? Who is that?" she asked startled.

"I figured you would play dumb with me." This time
he pulled the truck on the side of the road and sat staring
at her.

Alarmed and nervous from the intimidating pitch Ritz
used with her. "I'm serious I don't know no Trane."

His speech was harsh toward her. "Don't play fuckin'
dumb to me. Do I look stupid to you?" he asked, resting

against his window and cutting his eyes toward her.

"Was he at the party last night?" she asked, her voice timid.

"Yeah dat tall muthafucka from last night. Dat nigga said you gonna give him some. That ain't my problem if you do dats yo' business."

"I never said that to him. He assumed…" she was cut off by his menacing looks.

"It becomes my business when he is my enemy. I don't share business or women with that nigga."

"Like I said I don't know him and I never said anything like that," her voice shaken.

"Oh, I was just askin'. I don't do any type of business with him. He ain't my type of swagga."

"Who told you?" she asked nervously, looking over to him.

"He did. He was swearin' dat he had you eatin' out the palms of his hands."

She whispered, "He did tell me to drop you and get with him tho'."

"Once you do, you can forget about being my girl. I

don't play that shit."

"I didn't say I was. I'm your girl, Ritz."

"Dats what I like," he said and then kissed her on the lips.

He maneuvered the SUV back on the road and turned on some rap music. Janiece's fear slowly left her as she recognized the familiar scenery as they headed to the mall. It was only days away from her birthday. She had a lot to think about since she was about to turn the big one-eight. She wanted to spend her birthday with Jennifer, someone she knew who cared about her. As they strode inside the mall, they shopped. Ritz answered a phone call and stepped away. As she stepped inside a store, she heard her name called. She glanced over her shoulder and it was Jennifer.

"Sup girl, I haven't seen you in a while."

Acting shocked, Janiece replied, "Hey girl. I've been busy lately. What you been up to?" she asked Jennifer, gawking at her jumpsuit that flattered her curves perfectly.

"Workin'," Jennifer replied. "What about yourself?"

"Me too. Don' this and don' that."

Jennifer's eyebrows rose. "What you mean? Strippin'?"

"Nah girl," Janiece answered as she started walking toward Bombay, the shoe store.

"What then!" Jennifer demanded.

"You sho' is nosey."

Jennifer laughed. "He don't have you don' nothing that you said you wouldn't do, does he?"

"Nah girl." Janiece changed the subject. "How's the family? Your mama still workin' at the hotel?"

"Yeah the family is fine and she still workin'. But back to my question. What you don' to make money?"

"Since you so worried about me," she paused, "I sing and get paid."

Jennifer rolled her eyes, mockingly. "Who came up with that bright idea?"

"He did after findin' out I could sing."

"Really?"

"What?" Janiece asked with a smirk. "You act like he's bad or something."

"He is when he's sellin' drugs and pimpin' young girls."

Janiece felt insulted. "He ain't pimpin' me."

"I didn't say that but since you sound guilty, is he?"

"Nah, I'm his girl."

"And so are the other females I hear about. When you gonna leave that mess alone?"

"When I get enough money to take care of myself because…" Janiece stopped in mid-sentence.

"Yeah, I know. You can't go back home."

"I can if I want," she blurted out.

"My bad." Jennifer held her hands up. "I just heard around the neighborhood that your grandparents put you out."

"That ain't true," Janiece stated in a remorseful tone. She wished she could go back home and for everything to be like it used to be.

Jennifer asked. "What's the truth?"

"I left home. End of story."

"But if things get rough, you would go back home right?"

"I wish it was that simple. My grandma wouldn't let me."

"Even mean grandmas who love and miss their love ones would allow them back home. Don't be a fool out here too long 'cause it ain't worth it when you have a home."

"Did I ever tell you about my mama?"

"Nah you never did."

"Well, she died not too long ago because of drugs. Do you know how bad that tore me up? I saw in the newspaper one day that my mama was buried in June but I couldn't go to the funeral. I didn't want my grandparents to hassle me about moving back home or asking a whole lot of questions so I did us a favor and not show up. But as I think about it, I wish I would have gone to the gravesite at least. But I know I'm not mentally stable enough to see her now but I hope one day I can go out there and visit her."

"Girl, you funny. You better go back home before something really bad happens to you. You know what I'm sayin'?"

"Yeah but Ritz ain't like that," she didn't know why she felt she had to defend him against Jennifer because he sure didn't defend her when she almost got caught.

They left out of the store and sat down in the food court. "So do you call your grandparents?"

She shook her head.

Jennifer made a face. "They don't know if you're dead or alive?"

She shrugged her shoulders as she looked around the mall. She was keeping watch for Ritz.

"Why you ain't called them?" Jennifer asked wholeheartedly.

"I don't want to make them cry."

"But they'll be glad that you did even if you're just callin' to say hi. At least let them hear your voice. When was the last time you heard their voice?"

Janiece dropped her head. "The day I left."

"Which was?" inquired Jennifer.

"Six months ago."

"I don't know how you do it but I couldn't go a day without talkin' to mi madre," Jennifer exclaimed. "Call

146

them. It would make you feel a whole lot better and them."

"Yeah I will," was all Janiece said.

Janiece saw Ritz walking and jumped to her feet. She told Jennifer that she would call her later about her birthday ideas.

"Where you been?" he inquired, his voice harsh while studying her.

"I was sit-in' in the food court. I was waitin' on you," she said as they exited the mall. Later when she walked inside Mya's apartment, she was accused of stealing Ritz's money.

"I know you ain't holdin' out on Ritz. That man put you on your gig. He doin' you a favor. You ain't doin' him a favor. You're welcome, hoe. Now give me fifty dollars," Mya demanded.

"What're you doin' with the money?" she muttered as she strode down the hallway.

"What the fuck you say to me?" Mya uttered in a rowdy tone, springing to her feet and pulling her around to face her with her head shaking from left to right.

"Nothing," Janiece murmured.

Chapter 16

Pain is a pesky part of being human...feels like a stab wound to the heart... JoyBell C.

Janiece

Listening to a cheap MP3 player as she was walking up North Greenwood Street, Janiece quietly sang along to her favorite artist Keyshia Cole's *Let It Go*. She strode to the corner store. When she exited the store with her brown paper bag, it was still pretty light outside when she left. Inside her bag was Doritos, gummy bears, and a twenty-ounce cherry coke. She wanted to wait until she got to the apartment to enjoy the fruits of her labor when she noticed a black SUV parked on the opposite side of the road. She continued to walk down the sidewalk not paying too much attention to her surroundings.

A sudden movement caught her attention. She studied the dark suburban as it crept down the road. She didn't make eye contact. Something was off and she felt it. She felt like she was in the movie 'Home Alone' when Kevin was walking home from the store and the robbers were in their white van creeping up behind him. She hadn't prayed in a long time so she closed her eyes and said a quick prayer. Only three blocks from the apartment complex. The dark, tinted SUV slithered beside her. The SUV stopped. The back door opened. A tall brown-skinned man jumped out wearing a black ski mask. He grabbed her around the waist and covered her mouth with his hand. She didn't have time to scream. He pulled her inside. She kicked but it was no use.

Soon as the SUV sped off, the man who held her told her to be quiet. He covered her eyes with a black eye mask. He put masking tape over her mouth. At this point, she didn't know if she was going to live or die. She couldn't believe it. She had just gotten kidnapped. Why her out of all people? While inside of the SUV, she could hear voices but couldn't make them out. She felt another body sit beside her. She held her hands in her lap as she shivered. They rode for a while. Then the SUV came to a sudden halt. She heard the doors opening except for the one beside her.

"Don't you move, Lil pretty or it will cost your life,"

she heard the man's repulsive laugh.

She did as she was told. She didn't move. The man got out on the other side and left her in the truck. Voices were communicating on the outside of the vehicle. She couldn't hear what they were saying but she knew her life depended on listening to them or else. Just then the door on her side began to open.

"Get out real slowly," she heard a different man's voice.

Janiece, being blindfolded, stretched her legs outside of the car. A man reached out his hand and told her to grab his hands. She did and slid out of the vehicle. He grabbed her roughly around the arms and pulled her.

"Where are you takin' me?" she asked nervously, scared out of her wits.

"Bitch, ain't nobody asked you to talk," she heard another voice.

"Step up."

Right foot. Left foot. The sound of a creaky door caught her attention. She turned her head toward the right.

"Walk straight," the man said.

She put one foot in front of the other as she walked. She staggered in tiny steps. She didn't know where she was walking to. She just stepped. She strolled until she bumped into something. She felt around and it was soft. She figured it was a bed.

"Sit down," she heard the same voice.

Could my life be in danger? Will this be the last time I open my eyes for good? Did I run away from home for no reason? She thought before she felt the tears roll down her cheeks. *Jennifer tried to warn me that day but I didn't listen.* As she sat on the bed waiting for God knows what, she thought about her grandparents, Jennifer, her mom, school, and the good life that she had left behind.

She heard the door open and those slimy words. "Hey miss pretty."

She recognized the voice. *It was him.*

"You thought you could get away from me. Didn't your mama teach you about teasin' a man? When you tease, you get what you get."

"Trane?" she asked, a sob caught in her throat.

"Correct baby. I had to bring your sweet ass. You betta' not disappoint me. I gave up the streets for you tonight." His words were offensive. "You know I'm a businessman and time counts. Having you tonight is a good exchange for losing money and you betta' be just that, good. No, no. Not good but great."

"Why me? Why me?" asked Janiece as the tears poured from her eyes.

"That's the wrong question you're askin' but since you asked it's because you are sweet and precious just the way I like em'."

"Fuck you!

His laughter was haunting and sinister. "Yes, that's what I'll do to you in a minute."

"I'm a virgin. Please don't do this to me. I don't know how to do it. Please let me go and I'll forget about everything. About you kidnappin' me. I won't even go to the police if you let me go. I won't even tell Ritz."

"Funny that you mention Ritz. After I'm done wit you, he won't have anything to do with you," he declared, his laughter deadly.

"Please, please," she begged.

"I thought this would be a good reason to bring in your birthday," he said. "Now take off your clothes."

More sobs, she cried. "Please let me go. I won't tell. Let me gooo!"

She heard the shuffling of his feet as he inched closer to her. She then felt his grimy hands on the side of her face. She slapped his hand away.

"Ouch bitch, you like it rough? I'll show you rough. Now take off your clothes or I will."

Puzzled, Janiece sobbed as she started taking off her shirt.

"Wait. Stand up and strip for me," he commanded.

She did as she was told. Slowly. She took off her shirt not in a sexy way. She did it as if she was a helpless child. *Scared.* As she bent over, she kicked off her shoes in a flash. Why not do it in a hurry because she knew no matter what she tried to say, she couldn't talk him out of raping her? She put her hands on the button of her pants.

"Wait! Do it slowly and give me a dance when you take off those pants with those sexy ass hips."

She unbuttoned her jeans. Slid them off her slim hips. Kicked them off her ankles. She felt a closeness with the guy. She could feel his breath on her.

"You can take off that blindfold if you want."

"I'd rather not," she stated.

"But I want to see your eyes."

She sobbed.

"Okay, not right now because you'll mess up my groove."

Janiece now stood in front of Trane only in a matching bra and panties.

"How cute! Pink and white polka dots. All for me." His voice was deep and devilish.

Janiece felt him stand directly in front of her. She wanted him to hurry up and rape her. He knew what he was doing was evil. Hated him. For bringing her in the middle of nowhere probably and doing the unjust to her. His hands touched her cheek and lightly squeezed it. The stench of alcohol was offensive. Next thing she knew the wetness of his tongue slid up her face. He licked her tears. She felt disgusted now.

"Now take off my clothes," he said in his next breath. "You may want to take off that blindfold so you can see what're don'," he mused.

"Nooo," she uttered.

"Fine do it your way."

Being blindfolded, Janiece searched for his chest and found that the shirt didn't have any buttons on it. Although she wanted this awful situation to be over with, she wanted to prolong the actual raping. Closing her eyes, she sent up a silent prayer but didn't think it would do her any good.

"Fuck it, I'll do it. I want your pretty ass now," he said, taking off his shirt. He stepped back in front of her, grabbed her hand and placed it on the bulge of his pants.

"Ahhh," he moaned with pleasure.

She unzipped his pants and she heard him kick them off.

"I remember askin' you, what you did for some money," Trane chuckled. "You want something to drink before you get ripped open?"

Fuck, this was what life came to be. She gripped the

bottle, brought the tip of the bottle to her lips and gulped it. She cringed as the alcohol burned her lungs. She held the bottle out and felt him grab it out of her hands. With tears streaming down her cheeks, she felt around for the bed, sat down and scooted toward the center.

"Now I would ask for some head but I see you ain't never done it before and you ain't gone practice on me and bite my shit off. I'll go easy with you," he stated in a cunning, dark voice. "Take off your bra. I'll handle those panties of yours."

Drenched in tears, Janiece reached behind her back and unhooked her bra. Frightened and trembling, she lay consciously as Trane breathed heavily on her when he climbed on top of her. His heavy breathing irritated her but she had no choice. She lay there like a dead dog in the street. He moved toward her breast and started kissing her there before he grabbed her breast with one hand as he feasted on the other with his mouth. Janiece held her eyes closed even with the blindfold on. He alternated between sucking on the breast to grabbing them and twisting the nipples. She wanted to scream *get the fuck off me* but knew it would only excite him so she hushed. As she lay there, his hands started to roam down in between her legs.

Why me? Why me?

His fingers rubbed over her panties until he felt that it was moist. "Umm, I like that. I didn't know you could get so wet," he stopped kissing her breast and with one quick motion, he ripped her panties off. He tossed the ripped panties and maneuvered his nose toward her core. "You smell fresh just like a virgin."

Lying there without a fight, she felt dead so there was no need to struggle against his strong body. She felt his hands in between her naked legs. She felt her legs being pushed open roughly with his hands. She had no fight. She was already dead on the inside so it didn't bother her as much. He then grabbed both of her hands with his left hand and held them over her head. He shifted his body directly over her core and she felt his manhood grow larger.

"Condoms." It was more of a statement than a question.

"Nah, I go raw baby."

Twisting and turning, Janiece tried with all her might to get Trane off of her but it seemed like he liked it that way. He fought back too. With one thrust, he was inside of her. She flinched because of the pain. He broke her soul. Her faith. Her virginity. More tears flowed down her while she hurt and he pleased himself. Disgusted, hatred, sickened, nauseated, are all the things she felt while getting rape. *How she had it good? Why me?* She kept repeating to herself. Out of the blue, Trane started making strange noises. He started to buck. Then he said, "I'm about to cum," he quickly pulled off her blindfold and nutted onto her chest when he withdrew from her.

No expression but evil stared at her while his seeds spilled onto her chest. She couldn't move. Numbed and unresponsive, she stared at evil as he removed himself from her. She didn't look to see where he moved to. She just heard keys jangling and scuffling of shoes. She figured he was putting on his clothes.

"You might not want to report this to anybody because I know where your grandparents live," he indicated, his voice deadly.

Grandparents?

"By the way, happy eighteenth birthday," she heard him say before opening and closing the door behind him.

Chapter 17

Our present problems are small and won't last very long. Yet they produce for us a glory that vastly outweighs them and will last forever! 2 Corinthians 4:17.

Janiece

Janiece didn't know what time it was when she slowly sat up. Her hymen broke unintentionally because of rape. She ached. Pushed out of the bed. Stumbled from the soreness in between her legs. Onto the floor, the blood flowed. She picked up her clothes. Quickly put her arms through the shirt.

"Ouch," was all she said as she pulled up her pants.

No cell phone to call Jennifer or Mya so she had to walk. She walked out of the house and onto the dirt. Nothing looked familiar. She was out in the middle of nowhere at night.

On her journey back to the apartments, Janiece pondered crazy thoughts. *Did I deserve this? Maybe I did because I ran away from home. Maybe God hates me. Maybe God is punishing me. Why me. Why me?*

Walking poorly on the left side of the road, she spotted a block store on the right side. She knew she wouldn't go inside and ask the clerk what time it was because she felt ugly. She knew she looked like shit. And felt ugly within. She glanced at the store but continued to walk. A few miles ahead, there was a traffic light.

"I can do it," she muttered. She convinced herself that she could make it all the way back to the apartment. Soon she spotted some signs a couple of miles ahead. The signs read LaGrange nine miles. "Shit, I'm all the way out in the country somewhere," she cried.

Lights from a car pulled up beside her. A Caucasian guy rolled down his window and asked, "Want a lift?"

"No, get away from me!" she screamed.

"Excuse me. I was just tryin' to help," he said surprisingly as he pulled back onto the highway.

Traumatized, Janiece didn't want anyone to stop. All she wanted was to get to the apartment and she did. Stepping into the apartment because it wasn't locked, Janiece strolled in sideways and made it to her bedroom. She quietly shut the door behind her. At last, she could cry, rest, cry again and question herself why. A moment later, a knock came upon the door.

"You in there Janiece?" asked Mya.

She didn't answer. She hoped Mya would leave her alone because she wasn't in the mood.

"I know you in there 'cause I heard you come in. Open this damn door. I gotta talk to you."

Still, no answer as the tears fell.

"Open the fuckin' door. Derrell is on his way home."

Janiece sat up, walked to the door, and swung it open.

"What the fuck is your problem? Why you smell like that?" Mya asked question after question. "Why your clothes lookin' like that? Answer me? Where have you been? You in a whole lotta trouble. You know that right? Ritz wanted you to run something for him tonight."

Janiece tiptoed and sat in the middle of the bed with her back against the wall.

"For the last time, why you ain't answerin' me? You—" she was cut off from Janiece's outburst.

"I was raped!"

"Don't nothin' look like rape but—"

"Listen to me!" Janiece yelled. "Tra—"

Listen to you! Why the hell should I? No one listened to me. Mya eyed Janiece sickeningly. She rolled her eyes because telling only got her in trouble. So she did what naturally came and blamed the victim. "What the fuck? You tryin' to blame this on Trane. Oh, I heard what you've been don' lately. Now you want to blame this on him. I figured you would get into trouble like this with one of Ritz's enemies. Do you know how much he hates him? And then you play like he raped you. Get real, Janiece."

Janiece was sick and tired of listening to Mya's accusations. "I SAID, I WAS FUCKIN' RAPED and you don't believe me?"

Mya's chest tightened as she looked away before resting her eyes on Janiece again. *Don't nobody believe that shit when you tell 'em especially in the hood.*

"Can you please be a Lil' sympathetic towards me?" asked Janiece, bringing her knees in an upward position as she leaned down and wrapped her arms around her knees.

Suck it up, Janiece. It's all a figment of your imagination just like it was to me. Mya stood in front of her. "So you got raped. What the fuck am I supposed to do? I can't protect you."

"I wouldn't lie," she sobbed. "I can't go to the police."

"You right about that 'cause that will get all of us in trouble." Mya blew out an extended breath. "You know Ritz is gon' to be pissed."

"I know but it ain't my fault."

Mya smirked. "Shit, I believe they're on their way over here."

Janiece looked up worried. "You called them?"

"Yeah, I have no choice. Unlike you, this is my home. I gotta do what my man tells me to do," Mya stated heatedly. To Mya, Derrell was the one who showed her the game after she graduated from high school. He was her savior. Mya befriended Janiece for this purpose. To show her the rope of the game like the others before Janiece.

"You believe me, don't you?" Janiece cried as she

looked for Mya's support.

"Hey, you gotta do what you gotta do. I can't have your back and my man's too."

"So what're we gonna do?"

"Ain't no we bitch. There's you and you have to figure out a way. I'm sorry but I—"

"You ever been raped before?" asked Janiece.

Have I ever been raped? Fuck yeah! But shit, no one believed me like they won't believe you. Mya shifted her gaze to the side before answering in a low voice. "Yeah, but I had to keep livin'." Being rape was nothing anymore. Just something a person went through. Something swept under the rug. Mya learned that early in life. The only way to challenge life was by facing it like a strong person. To keep it moving.

Just then two voices came in the living room.

"Mya, Janiece bring y'all asses out here."

Janiece hid behind Mya as they both stood in the living room.

"What the fuck I hear you givin' your ass to that nigga Trane, Janiece? Didn't I tell you that I don't fuck with that nigga but you showin' yo' ass all over town? You couldn't wait to give him some. If losin' yo' virginity was that important to you then you should have told me and I could have given you anyone but you chose that nigga. And you know what that means? I don't deal with you no more, stupid ass bitch."

"I was raped, Ritz. You gotta believe me. I wouldn't do that to you on purpose," cried Janiece.

He folded his arms across his chest and held an intimidating stance. "Yeah right like I believe a fuckin' child."

Child? Is that what he thought of me? She pondered those thoughts for a moment. *What would happen to her now? Would she no longer be Ritz's girl anymore?* Thinking like a child, she should have been thinking more adult-like because before she knew it, Mya told her that she had to pack what she had and leave the apartment because she couldn't stay there anymore.

"Oh before you go, bitch, I found the money that you've been keepin' from Ritz," Derrell said as he handed Ritz two hundred dollars.

She was mortified to glare at Ritz but she did. The menacing look he held upon his face looked like he would slap the shit out of her. She turned to her friend Mya standing by the door. She hoped Mya would say something. She just dropped her head instead. There wasn't anything else to say. Janiece knew she had to leave at this point. Janiece backtracked to the room she occupied and gathered what little she had. What she couldn't fit into the bags she brought with her, she left it behind. Suddenly the door opened. Mya rushed in and gave her twenty dollars and told her about a shelter. She thanked Mya and left the apartment soon after. It was three in the morning and knew it was too late to bother Jennifer and her family at this time. So Janiece marched onto North Greenwood Street with her book bag and a large duffle bag around her waist. The tears clouded her vision when a car pulled up beside her. She jumped when she heard the engine nearby.

"I got a place for you Mami," a man's voice spoke.

Janiece shook her head and kept walking. The car sped off. Feet aching, she decided to take a break. She rested behind the corner store and sat down on the sidewalk. Reaching inside her coat pocket, Janiece reached in and pulled out the twenty-dollar bill Mya gave her. She stood up, tucked her bags tightly in a small corner of the building, and walked inside the store. She went straight to the back of the store and grabbed two drinks. She then walked up the potato chip aisle and grabbed a honey bun, Doritos, and a small bag of M&M's then to the front of the store. She laid all the contents on the counter without looking up at the cashier. The cashier told her nine dollars and sixty-seven cents. She then lay the twenty dollars on the counter while the cashier bagged up her groceries and gave her change. Walking out the door, she spotted a group of guys standing on the corner where she had her belongings. With wobbly knees, she stumbled around them. She grabbed her bags and put them around her waist. Two more hours and then she could catch the bus. *But where would she go?*

"Ay shawty, ain't you Ritz's girl?" a guy asked.

She dropped her head swiftly and trotted along the road. *Where can I go? I could go to Jennifer's. I could go back home and say I'm sorry but—*

Carrying the bags on her tiny body, her body started to feel the weight that was weighing her down. "A few more miles," she whispered. Janiece found a rundown house where people were standing outside. She walked up and a bunch of people in a huddle glanced her way for a moment and then went back to talking. Janiece saw a girl who looked to be around her age.

"Excuse me, what kind of place is this?"

The girl with a scowl on her face answered, "It's a hoe house. What else could it be?"

"Didn't know, that's why I asked," she stated shifting the heavy bags on her waist.

"Oh, you tryin' to be a smart ass."

"No, no. I was lookin' for a place to lie down for a couple of hours."

The girl looked at her friends and chuckled. "Yeah, that's what they always say and then get up and trick."

"Do you know who lives here so I could ask them?" asked Janiece as she stared at the girl.

"Yeah but it's gonna cost you," the girl said.

"Oh."

Janiece looked at the girl's out-stretched hand. She reached in her pocket and pulled out the change from the store and passed it to her. The grimace on her face suggested 'yeah you'll be back'. Janiece thanked the girl and roamed toward the brown house looking for the woman name Sugah.

"Umm, is that the new girl?" a man's voice asked.

Janiece hurried inside the house. A foul stench hit her in the nose. Her lips curved over her nose. It was a mixture of sex and cigarettes.

"You lookin' for someone," she heard a woman say.

"Yeah, I'm lookin' for Sugah."

Janiece glared at the dark-skinned woman who appeared no more than 5'8. The woman dressed in a Mumu with some red house slippers and a cigar hanging from her mouth.

"I'm Sugah. Let me guess, you want a room to rest?" she asked, tapping her foot.

Janiece nodded her head.

"You know it's gonna cost you," Sugah spoke in a

heavy accent.

"How much?" asked Janiece.

"How much you got?"

"Ten," Janiece lied to the woman because she had to keep some money for herself. Just like she lied to the girl she met outside, to Mya and Ritz. Her grandma told her a long time ago to always keep money on you just in case. Even if you have to lie and say, 'you ain't got no money'. The corner of her mouth curved recalling a positive tip her grandma shared with her.

"Ten? What ten dollars gonna get you?"

"Hopefully a couple of hours of sleep," was all she replied.

"Dis must be your lucky night because any other night I woulda charged you forty or you woulda to work to sleep here," Sugah answered in a Jamaican accent. "Since you have ten dollars, I'm gonna give you a blanket and a pillow."

Still standing in the same spot, Janiece said nothing as Sugah handed her the blanket and a pillow.

"Now follow me," Sugah spoke in a curt tone.

Janiece followed Sugah down the hall to a small room on the right. Sugah pushed the door open as Janiece passed by her and entered the room.

"Sleep tight. I don't cook for runaways unless you workin' for me." Sugah asked, "What time you plannin' to leave?"

"As soon as I get up."

"I guess I won't be able to see you but if you decide you need to work for money, you know where to find me."

The Middle

Chapter 18

A time to plant and a time to uproot.

Ecclesiastes 3:1

Janiece

Janiece heard noises coming from the outside of the bedroom. She stretched her limbs and sat upon the twin-size bed. She quickly grabbed her belongings before someone asked her for a favor. Opening the door, she found Sugah standing at the end of the hallway with two black women. The first woman had on skin-tight jeans and a tube top while the other sported tight shorts with fishnet stockings and a small jacket.

Walking down the hallway, Janiece mouthed a *thank you* to Sugah as the two women eyed her as she left with the bags on her back. She walked two miles to the nearest bus stop. The bus came right up after she did. As she climbed onto the bus and paid the fare, she sauntered to the middle of the bus and sat down. Looking up, she saw that it was ten in the morning. Quietly, she laid her head against the window. She knew where she was going. To

Jennifer's. The bus dropped off a load of people and she was one of them that got off on Alford Street.

She walked a few blocks to Jennifer's house but thankfully she didn't see her mother's car in the yard. She had second thoughts. She stalked toward the front door and the door swung open.

"What the hell happened to you?" Jennifer shouted hysterically, running over where she stood in the driveway of her house.

"I.. I—" was all she could utter.

Jennifer wrapped her arms around her. She didn't want to explain anything outside. No words were needed at the moment. It felt so good to be missed and wanted. Jennifer released her, grabbed a bag from her and told her to come into the house. She followed Jennifer as she dropped her bag in one corner of her room.

"Throw your bag down and come sit on my bed," she said. "Girl, what happened? Did they throw you out or something? Sit down."

Tears slowly fell from her eyes. "I can't. I need a bath."

"Okay, okay I'll go run you some water," she heard Jennifer say as she left the room.

Minutes passed by the time Jennifer walked back into the room while she stood in place and looked at her cautiously. She knew Jennifer had a thousand questions but first she wanted to soak in the tub. To forget about it a moment before she spilled her guts out to her.

"Hey, I left you a towel and washcloth on the toilet seat. Go ahead and I'll be here."

"Thank you, Jennifer," she uttered as her body began to tremble.

Jennifer hugged her once again and then told her to take her time in the bathroom. She nodded her head and left the room. Janiece slowly peeled the sticky clothes from her body. She stood over the tub looking down. The tears wouldn't stop falling. She blamed herself. How could she be so stupid and naïve? She climbed inside the water and sunk under the bubbles, getting her hair wet and all.

"Are you okay in there?" Jennifer asked with worry in her heavy accent.

"I'll be out in a minute."

Twenty minutes later she emerged from the bathroom with a towel wrapped around her body. She stepped inside Jennifer's room and she was nowhere to be found. Thankful for a few moments, she mused. She dressed quickly and then Jennifer walked in with a sandwich and a cup of Kool-Aid.

"Now have a seat on the bed."

Janiece took the cup and sandwich from Jennifer as she sat down on the bed. Still shaken from her previous night, Janiece started crying. She lifted her head and paused before speaking, "I...I was...I was raped," she stuttered.

Jennifer stood up so fast that she almost knocked over the cup in her left hand. "What did you say? Are you for real, for real?"

Janiece nodded her head.

"Tell me who and what happened. I promise you your secret is safe with me."

Janiece replayed the whole scenario as she heard the anger in Jennifer's tone as she paced around in her bedroom. She spoke both in Spanish and English.

"Oh my gosh, I knew it. I knew those people didn't mean you any good. I'm so sorry, Janiece. I wish you would've never experienced that," she said as she wrapped her arms around her and rocked her until she finished crying while Janiece held onto the sandwich and cup.

"You think your mom will be mad if I stayed here for a while?"

"Nah, you can stay here as long as you like," she replied. "But what about your grandparents? You think they won't be happy for your return?"

"I can't. I just can't right now."

"Okay, okay. I understand," replied Jennifer.

A week passed and Janiece was part of the family. She had daily chores such as taking out the trash, setting the table, helping Jennifer's brothers with their homework, and grocery shopping. Janiece finally felt like she fit in a family. No accusations or being criticized for not doing something specific in their eyes. Yes, she was with a family who loved her and she loved them.

179

Sitting on the back porch one day, Jennifer asked out of curiosity. "You think you ever gon' to press charges?"

Janiece jumped up out of her seat. "I can't do that. He will kill me and my grandparents. I can't," she cried.

"Okay, my bad. I just don't get it. When a girl gets raped, everybody sweeps it under the rug but I say tell it. Yeah, you were hangin' with the wrong crowd, but you didn't deserve this. Men like him need to burn in hell."

Janiece found that to be funny. "I know right," she agreed as she sat back down on the bench.

"Girl, we betta get in this house and clean it up before mi Madre gets home and starts cussin' in Spanish."

Things seemed to be going great until she spotted Mya, Derrell, Ritz, and his new chic on his arm walking into the Burlington Coat Factory department store. Janiece snatched Jennifer's arm and pushed her into Bath and Body Works.

"Ouch, that hurts. What's wrong with you?" she asked quizzically.

She didn't answer right away. She looked out in the

mall to see if she could see them. "Girl, I just saw them."

"Saw who?" Jennifer asked.

"Mya and dem."

"Where?"

"Gon' into Burlington," Janiece said in a raspy tone.

She asked Jennifer was she ready to leave. Jennifer nodded her head and they left. She saw her old crew laughing as they got into their vehicles. *A close call*, Janiece thought.

Seven Months Later

"I don't mean to sound so preachy or anything but I think you need to go home, Janiece," Jennifer said.

"What do you mean by that? I thought we were cool. You tryin' to give me a hint about puttin' me out? If it's your mom, I understand but I have to find a place to stay first."

"No," Jennifer said as she placed a hand on her shoulder. "I'm sayin' it as a concerned friend. I see how you look at mi Madre and my brothers. I just think you should return home to your grandparents. I know you will…"

"No! You have no idea what I went through while I was there. I can't go back there right now. Give me a few more months, please."

For the next few months, Janiece worked part time at the restaurant with Jennifer.

Chapter 19

Great is his faithfulness; his mercies begin afresh each morning. Lamentations 3:23.

Janiece

"Oh child, thank you Lawd," her Grandma said as she opened the door to see her standing outside with a Hispanic girl.

She was astounded to hear her grandma speak with joy toward her and then she saw her grandpa rushing through the door. She stood still and stared at her grandparents. She looked back at Jennifer to see what kind of expression beheld her face. It registered excitement. Her grandma stepped out and hugged her. She was shocked as hell. Her grandma hugged her so tight that her grandpa said, "You're going to squeeze her to death and I ain't hugged her yet." Her grandma let her go and then her grandpa hugged her and kissed her on the forehead.

"Come in, come in," Grandma repeated.

She and Jennifer stepped inside her grandparents'

house. Tears, joy, and thankfulness were what she saw on their faces. Her grandpa grabbed her duffel bags that lay on the ground.

There was silence as they stood in the living room, staring at one another. Jennifer stretched out her hands and introduced herself. "Hi, my name is Jennifer Gonzalez and I'm a friend of Janiece."

"Nice to meet you," they said in unison as they shook her hand.

"Janiece has been stayin' with me and my family for the past year. I've grown to love her like a sister. Uh, recently I told Janiece that she needed to return home and maybe pick up the pieces that she has longed for while she was on her own. I just want Janiece to be happy and feel like she is loved from y'all again. She didn't tell me what went wrong when she decided to run away a year ago," she stated. "I don't know maybe it's none of my business but I know that Janiece loves and miss y'all. I just thought that I should bring her home to y'all," Jennifer stated fervently.

Silence filled the room again until her Grandma

spoke, "Praise the Lawd."

Her grandma grabbed both of her hands and raised them to the sky. Her grandma was a tall woman and to see tears escaping from her eyes, shocked Janiece. She was in awe. Disbelief crammed inside her mind as she gawked at her grandma's behavior. A smirk hidden behind her eyes. Although it's been a year but she had to let the animosity go. Janiece glared at her grandma giving praise to the Lord.

"God brought my baby back home. Thank you, Jesus," her grandma said in a hoarse voice. "I'm so sorry Janiece. I hope you forgive me. I was mean and cruel to you. I should have known it would drive you away from me just like it did your mama. I was wrong and I admit I was wrong in the way I handled you. I just hope you can find it in your heart to forgive this old woman. I don't want you to ever leave me again. I love you too much to let you leave me. If it's in your will Lawd, punish me Lawd," she said as she raised both of their hands to the ceiling, thanking God for her many restless nights knowing her baby was out in the streets somewhere.

"You answered my prayers. All things work together for the good of those who are called according to your will," Grandma cited.

She turned to her grandpa who remained quiet until he stepped up and locked them in a bear hug. He had tears streaming down his face too.

"Honey, we are so glad you came home. We prayed many nights that he would bring us back together again."

She peeked through the corner of her grandpa's shirt and saw Jennifer shedding tears too.

"Should I go?" Jennifer asked momentarily.

"No, you're family."

Grandma then grabbed Jennifer into the group hug as she thanked God for allowing Jennifer to bring their grandchild home. After everyone calmed down, her grandma made some hot chocolate. They talked well into the night when Jennifer announced it was getting late.

"I gotta catch the late bus home."

"Why don't you spend the night since it's so late and I'll have my husband drive you home in the mornin' Jennifer?"

"Yes, ma'am."

"Call your mama first."

"Yes ma'am," she said as she used the house phone.

When Janiece awakened the next morning, the house smelled of breakfast food. After taking care of her hygiene and giving Jennifer a spare toothbrush, they trudged toward the kitchen and sat down. It was like old times. Her grandma was fixing everybody a plate of homemade buttery pancakes, scrambled eggs, sausage links, and a fruit salad. She also placed Aunt Jemimah syrup in the center of the table.

"Yum this looks and smells good," Grandpa uttered.

"Show'll do," the girls said in unison as Grandpa said grace as they ate in silence.

Soon as breakfast was over, Jennifer volunteered to help Janiece wash the dishes while her grandparents sat on the sofa and talked.

"I'm finished," Jennifer stated. "Remember what I said now. I'm still your girl and if you need anything I'm here."

"Thank you so much. You don't know how much that

means to me. You're like a sister I've never had."

"That's right! I am your sister but from another mother," they laughed in unison as they followed Grandpa to the car. Her grandma stayed behind while she rode with her grandpa to drop off Jennifer.

Her grandpa asked Jennifer where she lived and she told him. The way he said, "*Janiece, you were this close to home,*" broke her heart. It pained her to know she caused dissension and brought fear into their lives. She held her head down because it was a life lesson learned. The rest of the drive back home was quiet until the tunes to a familiar song began coming from her grandpa's tenor voice.

When they pulled up into the carport, her grandpa cut off the engine but didn't open his door. He hummed the song for a full minute before shifting in his seat to gaze at her. She knew it was going to be one of those talks so she braced herself.

"Janiece," he said. "Whenever you feel comfortable to tell me what happened in the streets, I'm here." His voice laced with sorrow and understanding.

She couldn't tell him ever. She didn't open her mouth. She dropped her head.

"Or if you don't ever want to talk about it, I'm fine with that too."

This time she looked up to him and smile with tears glistening in her eyes.

"Well, I'm glad that's settled. Let's go inside," he sighed. "I love you, baby girl."

"I love you too grandpa and I'm sorry," Janiece uttered.

"Hush that's water under the bridge now. We're just glad you're back," he said as he opened the car door.

She opened the door and met her grandpa as she walked around the car. He grabbed ahold of her and held her. She wrapped her arms around his waist.

"What're you giggling about?" he asked, carrying sorrow in his tone.

"Your tears are hittin' me in the face," whispered Janiece as she held onto his loving hug.

"Oh sorry, I thought I was being secretive but my tears thought otherwise. You see how emotions take over

189

like that?"

"Yes sir and I'm sorry for so much trouble I caused.
I'm sorry that I lived a few blocks away. I'm sorry I
didn't come home or call y'all. I'm sorry—" Grandpa
interrupted her.

"Let's finish this in the house. I don't want the
neighbors all up into our business," he said as he grabbed
her around the shoulders and led her into the house.

When they entered the house, they spotted Grandma
sitting on the sofa crying all over again. Janiece regretted
the decision she made and walked over to her Grandma
and hugged her.

"I'm sorry for runnin' away like I did. I know you
didn't need another heartache after how my mama left but
I— I'm sorry for causin' your pain. I do love you and I
promise I'll do better if y'all give me another chance. I
want y'all to forgive me."

"Hush child, all things are forgiven. You're home
now. I'm sorry for the way I treated you. I had no right,
sugah. Grandma is sorry. Do you forgive me?"

"Yes, ma'am."

They grinned in unison. "I see you still got some manners."

"Yes ma'am, I do."

"Now let this be all water under the bridge. If you want to do right, then we will help you."

"Thanks, Grandma."

"What about me?" her Grandpa asked.

"You too Grandpa. I love y'all so much and I'm grateful to have y'all in my life."

Grandpa said. "Now what're your plans?"

"To get my diploma and to go to college."

Over the next weeks, Janiece was back into the swing of things. She did her daily chores, researched information on how to take online classes to get her high school diploma. Janiece received her high school diploma in five weeks. When her nineteenth birthday came around, she treated it like another day. Nothing to celebrate. It took her two years to enroll in college.

By September, she walked across the campus of LaGrange in search of her first class. It was Biology. But before she could think straight, her stomach growled forcefully. She held her stomach in but it rumbled again. To hell with it, she went in search of food.

Chapter 20

When you are a new creature in Christ, all things are anew; the old has gone...2 Corinthians 5:17.

Janiece

Dang, I don't want to eat lunch by myself, she mumbled. *Shoot, I may have no choice today.* Janiece wandered inside the cafeteria. She pulled out her school ID and swiped it under the laser. It beeped. The laser read the barcode. Her eyes landed on an empty table on the left. She strolled over and placed her book bag down. Walked in line and grabbed a tray. Placed a plate, fork, spoon, and napkins on top of the tray.

She stared at the young woman whose complexion was of a medium bronze color with a cute, short hairstyle in front of her. She stood 5'7 inches tall. Just two inches shorter than her. She looked like she weighed one hundred and sixty pounds. The young woman turned around and said, "Do you know if their Chicken Tetrazzini tastes good?"

"I don't know. This is my first time eatin' in here,"

was all Janiece replied.

"Oh, I hope it's good then."

Janiece told the lady that she wanted the baked chicken with a side of green beans and rice. She also grabbed a handful of chocolate chip cookies and a glass of Sprite. As she headed back to her table, she found the same girl sitting there. Janiece knew that no table was promised to a person just because your book bag was there. Janiece stopped in front of the table. She reached down for her book bag. The girl who was sitting down at the table looked up.

"Oh, I'm sorry. I didn't know you were sitting here. You can sit here unless you wanna sit somewhere else," the young woman responded.

"Thanks, I'll sit here."

The young woman seasoned her food and then told her that her name was Shaneema. "What's your name?" she asked in return.

"Janiece," she replied. "You live on campus?"

"Nah, I live at home with my two kids. Whata 'bout you?"

Two kids, she didn't look a day over twenty-one, Janiece thought. "How old are you?" she asked skeptically.

"Twenty-three," she replied. "You?"

"Twenty-one." Still shocked by her answers. She asked, "How old are your kids?"

"My oldest is eight and my youngest is three," she answered as she seasoned her food with the pepper on the table.

Shocked, Janiece tried to figure out in her head what age Shaneema had her first child. "So that must mean that you had your first child at fifteen."

"Yeah, yeah, I know. It was hard but I had my mama's support too. It's a blessin' to have kids. Do you have any?"

Janiece shook her head.

"Good. Don't get none no time soon 'cause they're a lot to handle," she replied as they continued to engage in small talk as they ate their food.

Janiece looked at the time, "I gotta go to my class. I'll see you later, Shaneema. It was nice meetin' you today.

Hopefully, it won't be our last," Janiece said as she gathered her tray and book bag.

"Girl, it won't. You got class tomorrow?"

"Yep."

"I'll see you same time tomorrow."

This is how they met up with each other every day between twelve and one for lunch. If not lunch, then it would be the library, the mailbox, or at the small diner on campus.

Beginning of November, Janiece was walking toward the library to meet up with Shaneema when a suave, chocolate complexion man with a high-top fade walked up to her.

"Hey, sexy Mami."

"Hi," she said as she kept walking.

He sprinted in front of her. "Whoa, where are you off to in a rush?"

"To the library," was all she replied as she kept walking.

"You look like the smart kind. What're you?"

Suddenly she stopped walking and stared at him.

"What do you mean?"

"Junior, a sophomore?" the guy asked.

"Freshman."

"Really? You look more like a sophomore."

"But I'm not. You're makin' me late," she said as she tried to step around him but he cut her off with his steps.

"I just wanted to see a beautiful face before I went off to class. You gonna be around later?"

"Nope," she said as she started her steps again. When she entered the library, her friend was waiting for her at the computer desk.

"Girl, what took you so long?" Shaneema asked sitting at the computer desk, removing her books from the reserved computer she saved for her.

"Girl, this dude was tryin' to holla but I ain't have time for him."

"I know that's right." Shaneema paused. "You don't need no nappy-headed boy 'cause you got an education to get."

"I hear ya on that," Janiece replied and high-fived her friend. They stayed in the library for two hours working on assignments. Then they both left the campus and met up at the mall.

"What're you don' for Thanksgiving break?" Shaneema asked.

"I'll be around the house with my grandparents. Maybe I'll invite my friend Jennifer over. Why? What're you up to?" asked Janiece.

"My kids are gon' with their fathers. I was gonna chill at my mom's."

"They have the same daddy?" she asked.

"Nah, I wish. My oldest child's dad lives in Decatur. We were high school sweethearts. When I told him I was pregnant, he left. He told everybody that I was sleepin' around and stuff. Him being stupid. My youngest baby daddy lives here in LaGrange but we don't talk unless it deals with my baby boy. He married this girl from Augusta and I can't stand her. She acts like she all that because she married him. She must don't know that I was there first. But anyway, that's old news. I'm not tryin' to talk to any more men unless they got something gon' for themselves. A job, money, and a roof over their head.

Girl, it's all about me, my boys and my education," she sighed.

"I know that's right."

They studied for another hour before they went their separate ways.

Chapter 21

Pleasant words are a honeycomb, sweet to the soul and healing to the bones. Proverbs 16:24.

Janiece

Mid-November, Janiece was dressed in black pants and a pink sweater as she strutted to her Spanish class. She saw a striking guy. He was tall and had a mocha complexion. He sported a low haircut and a muscular build underneath his baggy pants, brown sweater and Timberland boots. As he was walking in the opposite direction with his boys, he did a double look at her. She had a feeling that he would try to holler at her and when he left his friends and sauntered in her direction, she guessed right.

"How're you don'?" The guy stopped in front of her. "My name is Lyric."

She ignored him.

"You ain't gonna stop. So you're just gonna keep on walkin' huh?" he asked.

"Yeah gonna be late for my class," she stated. As she

walked, she thought about Shaneema not showing up for lunch and knew she needed to get a cell phone. "What do you want? I have to go to class."

"Chill," he said as he jogged alongside her fast pace walking. "I just want to know your name is all. If you must know I'm at the top of my class, I'm majorin' in Biology. I have no kids and I don't intend to have any until I'm married," he rushed out.

She halted her steps. "What're you gon' for?"

"I'm gonna be an engineer one day," he stated. "What about you?"

She looked down at her watch. "I'm undecided about my major."

"Jason Lyric Shaw. And yours?"

"Janiece Turner," her mind registered that he was going somewhere in life and plus he wasn't bad looking either. From that moment on, they got to know each other and then began dating. Of course, she didn't tell her grandparents about him yet but there would be a time, just not this one.

Sitting down at the dinner table, Janiece said grace.

After everyone caught up on their events, Janiece asked her grandparents if she could get a part-time job.

"What about school?" Grandpa asked.

"Since I have mornin' classes, I can afford to get a part-time job."

"The mall would probably be a good place for you to start," her grandma suggested.

"No!" Janiece shouted. "Sorry," she said as she saw the expression on their faces. "I was thinkin' that I would get a job elsewhere. So can I?"

They looked at each other first and then her grandma said yes. Within two weeks, Janiece was working at AT&T; the cell phone store. She knew if she worked there that she could get a discount on a cell phone. Soon enough she got herself a Samsung camera phone.

After Thanksgiving break, she and Lyric spent a lot of time together. He lived on campus. She was invited but she declined every time. One afternoon, she walked out of his dorm building. She heard her name being yelled out and glanced over her shoulder. It was Shaneema running in her direction.

After catching her breath, Shaneema asked. "Hey, girl. I called your name but it seemed like you were occupied. Who's your friend?"

With a huge grin upon her face, she answered. "Lyric. We're newly datin'."

"You're not havin' sex with him, are you?" Shaneema asked worriedly.

"No!"

"If you are, I hope you're usin' condoms. You don't want no babies, Janiece. You don't need that right now. And he's still in school. He'll dog you out. Right now he might be tellin' you he loves you and all. Just don't get played, that's all I'm sayin'," reprimanded Shaneema.

"I'm not havin' sex with him," she said exasperatedly. "I can't."

"What you mean you can't?"

"It's a long story."

"I got time," stated Shaneema, lifting her eyebrows at her. "My next class isn't until three."

Janiece found a booth as they sauntered inside of their

school café while Shaneema stood in line to order something from the menu. The small, intimate café served hotdogs, hamburgers, fries, and sandwiches off the grill.

"Girl, we've been friends since when? Since beginnin' of this semester so I know you can trust me. Did I not tell you my business?" asked Shaneema.

Janiece nodded her head.

"Well, you can tell me. Let's go to my car if you want. I'm not parked far," she said as Janiece followed her toward her '03 silver Toyota Corolla.

Janice sat on the passenger side of the car. Shaneema turned on some music but kept it low. "Well?" she turned to face Janiece.

Janiece twitched and twisted her fingers awhile before opening her mouth. "Well, the only person who knows about this is my friend Jennifer. It's too painful," she said as the tears began to fall.

"I'm sorry. Maybe you're right," Shaneema stated as she put down her fries. "You don't have to tell me."

"No, it's okay. I feel safe enough to tell you. You're

my other best friend now."

"Thanks, girl. Your secret is safe with me."

"Well, my mom died of drugs when I was seventeen. I ran away from my grandparents to live with who I thought was a friend and her boyfriend. I ended up hookin' up with one of his friends. Oh, I forgot I was still a virgin at the time," she said suddenly. "Ritz had me making drops and he rewarded me by taking me shopping, or out to eat or give me cash. Then after he found out that I could sing, he had me singing for money. I was paid by the club owner and was supposed to give him all the money I made but I wasn't that stupid. I learned from my grandma to always hold money back. And I did. Gave him what I thought he should have along with giving my ex-friend Mya some change on the side from time to time. Anyways, we had parties all week long. I didn't contact my grandparents at all while I was living with them. I was out one-night walking back to the apartment from the corner store."

Shaneema inquired, "Which corner store?"

"It's not important," Janiece stated as she sat forward,

not looking at her.

"You're right. Finish your story."

"A black SUV pulled up beside me, I tried to ignore it but they stopped and next thing I knew I was in the back seat of their car."

Shaneema hollered. "They kidnapped you!"

"Yeah. Anyways I was taken out of town to an abandoned house where he raped me on my eighteenth birthday."

Shaneema gasped. "I'm so sorry to hear that. Now I'm mad. Told you not to tell me but I'm glad you did. Did you press any charges?" she asked throwing her arms around Janiece.

"Nah."

"Why not?"

"Because he knew where my grandparents lived."

"Shit, my bad that made me cuss." Shaneema stared at her with wide eyes. "Does the guy live here?"

"They all do. So I was kicked out by my friend's apartment and stayed with my friend Jennifer and her family until she told me that it was time for me to go back home. And I'm here don' me."

"Yes, you are. Oh wow, girl. You've been through something but you are strong." Shaneema expressed fervently. "But are you okay, mentally?"

"So far as I know," she joked.

Chapter 22

Have mercy on me, O God, according to your
unfailing love...Psalm51:1.

Janiece

For Christmas, her grandpa told her to get his hat out
of his car. Janiece glared at her grandpa oddly. *Now, why*
would he need me to get his hat out of his car at eleven
o'clock in the morning? It was suspicious but she was
going to do what her grandpa asked of her. She put on a
big jacket and shoes. She grabbed his truck keys and
sauntered outside.

A red '99 Honda Accord was sitting in their
driveway. She tiptoed to her grandpa's truck and opened
the door. She looked inside but didn't find his hat. The
red car piqued her interest. She had a moment of a
flashback. She dashed back inside and shouted, "There's
a red car in the driveway."

Her grandparents stood in the middle of the family
room with smiles on their faces.

"Why are y'all lookin' like that? It's a red car

outside," Janiece stated again.

Grandpa reached into his back pocket and pulled out some keys. "No one's here. It's your Christmas present."

"Really?" she shouted. She walked over and grabbed the keys. "Are you serious?" she questioned again.

"Yes, go on out there and take a drive."

"I will soon as I put some clothes on," she hugged her grandparents and thanked them repeatedly. "Thanks, Grandpa and Grandma. Oh my gosh, I have a car. Thank you, Jesus!"

"That's right call on Jesus!" her grandma shouted.

Janiece jumped up and down happily. She couldn't believe her eyes. She turned to face them before running off to put on clothes. "Can I bring my boyfriend over for dinner one day?"

"Boyfriend? This is the first time I'm hearin' about this," her grandpa exclaimed, his smile turning into a frown.

"Me too," her grandma stated.

"How long have y'all been dating?" he asked.

"A few months."

"How you manage to keep that away from us?"

"Well…" she stated.

Her grandpa gave her that serious look and put his hand on his hip.

"Well, I didn't want y'all thinkin' nothin' strange like y'all don' now."

"Thinkin' what?" her grandpa questioned joking. "If this young fellow passes my test, then he might end up marrying you."

"I'm not ready for no marriage. I have school to worry about."

"And no baby either," her grandma chipped in.

"I know," she said as she sauntered into her room. She quickly picked up the phone and called Jennifer and Shaneema. She told Jennifer to be ready at twelve because they were going out. She called Shaneema but she couldn't find a babysitter so she couldn't go for a joyride.

The next day, she met up with Lyric at Days Inn. She knocked on room 203. He opened the door in shorts and nothing else. "Hey beautiful, how was your Christmas?"

"It was good. My grandparents bought me a car," she said as he kissed her on the lips.

"What! Go ahead now. You took your girls for a joyride?" he asked as he grabbed her hands and led her to the bed.

She stopped in front of the bed and glared at him. "I took Jennifer yesterday because Shaneema couldn't come."

He guided her hand as they sat on the bed. All they did was chill. He asked her to spend the night with him in the hotel but she declined. For starters, she wanted to show her grandparents that she could be trusted again. Second, she wasn't ready to be intimate with another man so soon. He told her that he had a room for tomorrow night also. She told him that she would come back to see him.

She returned to the hotel room the next day around noon. He took her out to eat. When they came back from Applebee's, they chilled. Sitting on top of the bed, his hands began rubbing her back. And then her shoulders.

She tensed under his touch.

"I just want to make you feel good," his breath smooth.

She wasn't feeling the vibe. "I thought we were gonna chill."

"We are." He pulled on her shoulders. "Come on and lean back on the bed and get your mind off on whatever that's botherin' you."

"I'm good," she replied.

"I thought you liked me," he started to kiss her on the neck. "Are you gon' to spend the night tonight?"

"I have church," she lied.

"I'm gonna start thinkin' that you don't like me anymore," he whined.

"I do like you a lot," she added.

He kissed her neck and whispered, "I just wanna make love to you."

Janiece shook her head and sat up in bed, not looking at him.

He cupped her chin and turned her face to him. "Baby, I'm sterile. It means I was born with no sperm in my body."

Janiece cut her eyes at him in question. "What do you mean?"

"It's some shit called a zoo sperm something. All I know is that I can't get you or no other female pregnant. I've tried on many occasions." His breathing rough.

She shrugged her shoulders. "I don't know, Lyric. I don't want to disappoint my grandparents. I'm tryin' to be a better person."

"You can," he cooed as he laid her down on the bed. "You have nothing to worry about," he professed.

"I don't know, Lyric," she moaned his name as he kissed his way down her body.

"Don't worry, ma. I got you," was all he said as he fucked her without a condom. "Damn, your pussy is good."

During their lovemaking session, her heart raced. It felt like the last time. It scared her. Crazy thoughts roamed through her mind as he panted above her as he released his semen inside of her.

Two months later.

"Hey girl, you're not eat in' lunch today," Shaneema

asked by nudging her with her elbow as they sat on the bench outside of the cafeteria.

"Nah, I'm not hungry," she replied holding her pre-nursing book in her lap. "I'm tryin' to study for my Microbiology finals in an hour."

"Oh, well I'm hungry," Shaneema announced again. "So you want to come inside the lunchroom and I'll help you study?"

"No thanks. It's noisy in there but you can eat and I'll be out here if you want to help me when you finish," she said without looking up.

"Okay." Shaneema stood up this time and looked down at her. "Girl, what's really gon' on? I've never seen you stressed over a test like this before. You usually have everything done. You mean to tell me that you didn't have time to study last night?"

"Uh, uh," was all she said.

"Well, I'm gon' in to eat and if you're still out here then I'll help you."

"Okay."

"You ready?"

Caught off guard, Janiece quickly wiped her eyes. "Yeah, one minute."

Janiece waited for Shaneema to take her seat beside her before she handed her the notes. As Shaneema was quizzing her, she answered every question correctly.

"Girl, you know every answer on this page. What's up?" questioned Shaneema.

Janiece shrugged her shoulders without responding. She glanced around at then stared at her friend. Shaneema then asked her where her boyfriend was and she said around.

"Uh, uh somethings wrong," she announced. "What'd he do?"

"I don't want to talk about it."

"The hell you do," Shaneema said as she twisted her neck. "You actin' funny. Let's go somewhere and talk."

Janiece blurted, "I think I may be pregnant."

"No the hell you don't!" Shaneema paused and faced her.

"My period is late."

"Has that ever happened before?"

215

"No, I'm always regular."

"You took a test yet?" asked Shaneema.

"I'm scared."

"Well after your final and my last class we're gon'."

A few hours later at Shaneema's apartment, they both looked down at the Clearblue digital pregnancy test, *'pregnant'*.

"Shit, what am I gon' to do?" Janiece cried. How could she be pregnant? She didn't want this. She was doing well in school and life was throwing her a monkey wrench.

"Raise your child," Shaneema said sternly.

"But I'm twenty-one and a sophomore. I'm still livin' at home."

"Yeah, but you knew what you were don'."

"They gon' to hate me, they gon' to hate me," Janiece sobbed heavily.

"Hush girl, its gon' to be alright. Your grandparents ain't gon' to hate you. They probably wanted you to finish school. Don't sweat it. You will have help."

"I can't, I can't," she wept.

Friday afternoon Janiece shook her legs as she waited in the health department. Janiece looked up when the nurse called her name. Her head pointed down as she walked in shame. She followed the nurse into the back room. The nurse had her pee in a cup. She was led into a room. Minutes later the nurse popped her head in the door and gave her a brown bag of prenatal vitamins.

"Chin up, you'll pull through," was all the nurse said as Janiece walked out the health department.

Sitting in the passenger seat in Shaneema's car, she rode in silence as she thought about who to tell next.

Chapter 23

Create in me a pure heart, O God, and renew a steadfast spirit within me. Psalm 51:10.

Janiece

She dialed Lyric's number. He answered on the first ring. "What's up? How come I haven't heard from you in a while?"

"Funny that you should ask," Janiece joked, trying to keep it in a playful tone. "We need to talk now."

"Okay, come to my apartment," he said in a hesitant tone.

Ten minutes later, she knocked on his door while Shaneema waited in the car. He opened the door in pajamas and a wife beater. He kissed her on the forehead as he held the door open. She walked to the left side of the apartment which led into his bedroom.

"What's up?"

She blurted out, "I'm pregnant."

He quickly jumped off the bed. "It ain't mine."

Her face turned beet red. *Lyric is lying.* "I thought you

said you couldn't get me pregnant."

"I know and that's why I said it ain't mine."

"You buggin', Lyric. This is your baby. I didn't lay down and get this baby by myself."

"I mean how do you know for sure?"

"My friend and I just left the health department and it came back positive," she said, pulling out the white bottle of pills. "See, they have me takin' these big prenatal vitamins."

The color in his face flushed. "Uh, uh," he said. "What're you gon' to do about it? If you want, I can take you somewhere and get—"

"What the hell? I'm keepin' my baby. So that's it. You're ready to get rid of it," she smacked her lips. "Did you say that while you were beatin' it up? Hell nah! As I quote you said, 'Oh baby, this is good. You got that good pussy.' You remember that, you piece of shit?"

"Whoa, calm down!" he stated holding his hands in the air.

"I am calm! Whether or not you want to be in this baby's life, I am gonna need your support."

"You mean money? That's what all the sluts say."

"Slut? I got your slut," she twisted her neck. "How could I be so stupid in believing you cared for me? First my mother and now you!" she hollered.

"Keep that shit down." He stepped closer to her. "I don't want my roommates hearin' our conversation."

"I don't care what they hear," she said, knocking over his CD tower as it crashed to the floor making a clanging noise as she stormed out of his bedroom. She opened and slammed the door to his apartment-style dorm.

Later that day

After Shaneema dropped her off, she took a nap. When she awakened for work, she realized she hadn't told Jennifer her news yet. Janiece put her work clothes on. She had a few hours till work so she stopped by Jennifer's house. She jumped out of the car and rang the doorbell repeatedly.

Jennifer opened the door wearing sweatpants and a tank top. "Hey girl, what's up?"

"I'm pregnant," was all she said before entering the house with Jennifer trailing behind her.

"Well, it's time to tell them."

"I agree because I don't want to start my comeback with lies," she stated as she braced herself soon as she stepped in the house with Jennifer trailing behind her for support. She inhaled a sharp breath.

Her grandpa was the first to look up from the news. "What's wrong 'Neece? I thought you had to work?"

She opened her mouth but closed it. She started to speak again and fear caught in her throat. She cut her eyes at Jennifer when she felt a nudge on her back.

"I…I'm pregnant," she whispered as she dropped her head.

"You're pregnant?"

"'Neecee, you know you have to finish school. This baby ain't gon' stop you from your education. We won't have that, you understand?" her grandpa stated in a calming tone.

Janiece lifted her head in surprise. She knew her grandparents were going to renege on their offer to help her.

"How far along are you?"

"Uh…uh, I'm five weeks."

"Who's the father?"

"A guy I met at college but he said he didn't want anything to do with the baby," she cried.

Her grandpa closed the gap and wrapped his arms around her. "That's a damn shame. Men out here makin' babies but ain't takin' care of them. I don't know what's wrong with the youth." He shook his head. "Well, if he won't do it, then I will help you 'Neece but we'll help anyway we can," he looked over to his wife. "I will rent you out of a one-bedroom apartment. I will pay for your utilities as long as you can follow these rules."

She nodded her head.

"I want you to promise that you'll finish school, continue work if you can and no men."

"Yes sir, I promise. Thank you so much because I feel like a failure. I'm sorry," she cried harder in his arms.

"But you have to provide your own groceries," her grandma said.

Long after Jennifer left, there was crying and gnashing of the teeth. All in all, Janiece was blessed to have grandparents like she did. She was thankful that they stood on their word to help. She had to provide for the food which wasn't a big deal because she was going to get food stamps.

She knew her grandparents were disappointed with her setback. She could only hope to continue all the things she promised her grandpa, unlike her mother.

It was November eighth at 1:06 p.m. when the doctor told Janiece to push. "It's time Janiece," the doctor exclaimed. "I want you to push now."

Janiece took a deep breath and pushed at the bottom of her pelvis as the nurse counted to ten. Janiece continued the pushing while the nurse continued the counting. Between all of that, Janiece was crying, sweating, and cursing under her breath.

"Come on girl, you can do it," she heard Jennifer say.

"Yep, you got it," another voice said.

When she looked up, it was Shaneema. Janiece invited both of her grandparents into the hospital room with her but they declined and told her that Jennifer and

Shaneema would take their place. They wanted to wait in the waiting room. Within seven hours of labor, Janiece gave birth to an eight-pound and three-ounce baby girl. Janiece and her baby were released from the hospital three days later. Her baby took some of its colors from her dad. She was a big ball of almond joy with a head full of curly black hair.

"You did good girl. Look at you don' grown woman-ish," Shaneema uttered as she glared at Janiece.

"I know right," Janiece uttered through sleepy eyes.

"We'll watch after the baby while you get some rest," Jennifer stated, looking over to Janiece as she lay in bed.

"Ok," was all she said before she dozed off.

Two hours later when Janiece woke up, her best friends were in the living room as she emerged from her bedroom.

"How're you feelin'?" asked Shaneema.

"I'm still a little sore. Do you know where those Percocet's are?" asked Janiece.

"I'll get them for you. How many do you need?" she asked.

"Two 'cause I'm in pain."

"Well, you need to go back to bed. Your baby will be okay. We got you."

Her heart swelled with adoration how her two best friends took care of her. Unlike Mya, they were her girls/homegirls/besties because they cared and showed love. "Thanks, y'all are a big help. If I didn't have y'all, I wouldn't know what to do," she started tearing up.

"Uh, uh, we don't need no more cryin'. Bye Janiece," Jennifer stated.

Janiece held out her hand as Shaneema placed two Percocet's and gave her a glass of water. Before walking out of her bedroom door, Shaneema announced over her shoulder that she was making spaghetti. It lasted a week. She couldn't believe all things were working out for her good after all. A lonely tear started to form but she quickly blinked her tear away. When she awakened an hour later, she sat up in bed and glanced around the room and found her baby girl sleeping in the bassinet that her grandpa bought her.

Her baby's first Christmas Janiece dressed her

daughter in a pretty, chiffon red dress with black patent leather shoes. For the holiday, Janiece and her family traveled to Thomasville, Ga to visit some relatives. She had fun with her small family. It was a blast. It felt good to be back at home.

Janiece went back to school in January. She decided to pursue a nursing degree. She was a sophomore. She also worked at AT&T to support herself and her daughter. Her grandparents helped her out by babysitting her daughter while she was in school and working. For the nights that she didn't have to work, she would stay later at her grandparents' house to enjoy their company. On days to give them a break, Jennifer volunteered to watch her baby since she was the god mama. For her no-good baby daddy, she didn't get anything from him. He had signed over his paternal rights. Grandpa stepped in as the father.

"Are you gon' to tell Lyric that he's a proud daddy of a beautiful baby girl?" asked Jennifer.

"Nope, he gave up his rights a long time ago when he didn't want any part of us. I'm happy to say that I'm happy about my life. I know my grandparents love me no matter what; especially my Grandma. I thought she was gonna trip for real when I told her about the baby. Y'all don't know her like how she used to be. It's bad to say but I was just ready for the altercation between us. I thought she was gonna backslide on her words and try to put me out. But she really shocked me tho. I know it's crazy but hell I was kinda looking for the disagreements and stuff," she stopped talking and looked over at her friend. "That's crazy, huh?"

"Girl, you crazy. Didn't your folk's say they were sorry that one time?" inquired Shaneema.

"Yeah, I know my grandpa had a lot of say when it came to letting me stay in the house until I was in my last trimester. I know my grandma wanted so badly to say something negative to me but she held out and I was shocked. I just knew she was gonna say that I was just like my mama."

"But you're not. You're a strong, black woman who has chosen to raise your baby, continue school and work, shall I say. You know that's hard to maintain when

227

you're a young woman taking on the world by herself," replied Shaneema.

"Yeah, but I only work on the weekends."

"That's still good," Shaneema exclaimed fervently. "Because you know that's hard and even harder when you're don' it by yourself with no help."

"Maybe that's what my mama thought. She was don' everything by herself."

"Sorry sis, but no. Your mama had help but she refused to accept it."

"I know, I know. I just wished I would have seen her before she died." Janiece's voice cracked. "As I think about it, she knew where I was stayin' but if she cared, she would have gotten me a long time ago."

"Nah, I don't think you wanted to be in those drug houses with her," responded Jennifer as they were sitting down at her apartment having girl talk.

"At least…I don't know. I think she took the easy way out of life by takin' her own life. She could have quit a long time ago if she loved me," she verbalized as tears began pouring from her eyes.

228

Shaneema wrapped her arms around her. "That's right. Get it all out."

Chapter 24

He heals the brokenhearted and binds up their wounds.

Psalm 147:3.

Janiece

Four months later

Sitting at her computer desk typing a paper for her Physics class, she glanced down at her daughter playing with a toy sitting in her playpen. She studied her daughter for a long time. *God, I am so thankful that you let me have her. I did have problems at the beginning of my pregnancy but Lord you saw me through and I am so grateful. Thank you, Jesus!* She mumbled. After giving God the praise, she busied with her paper.

Janiece didn't finish typing her paper until late in the morning. In between the typing, her daughter was fussy. When she laid her down for bed, she felt that her daughter was a bit warm. She left the room to retrieve some Motrin but when she returned her daughter was sound asleep. On Tuesday morning, Janiece dropped her daughter off at her grandparents while she went to class. She met up with Shaneema at lunch. Soon as they left the cafeteria, she saw Lyric talking to another girl.

Shaneema interrupted her thoughts. "Girl look at him. He is so triflin'. You know he probably gonna get her pregnant too. I think we should go over there and cuss his ass out."

"Girl stop trippin'! I am so through with him that I don't have anything to say to him," she said as they walked passed Lyric. The girl he was talking to was another light-skinned girl but she had long golden locks.

She parted ways with Shaneema and walked inside the administration office to talk with her advisor. Her advisor advised her to start applying for the nursing program as soon as she passed the TEAS test. Janiece nodded her head. She left out the advisor's office feeling good. *Life was great*, she thought as she strutted toward her car.

All she had to do was pass the nursing exam to get admitted into the nursing program. She set a date in June. Hopefully, by fall she would be in the nursing program.

As she started her car, she drove to work. Her song *'Crazy'* by Gnarls Barkley came on. She sang the lyrics and bobbed her head to the rhythm.

"Maybe I'm crazy, crazy probably," her melodious voice sang in tune.

She turned into the parking lot of AT&T. Another one of her songs came on before she got out of her car. She walked into her job and went straight to the back. Some customers had walked in when she emerged from the back. She assisted them and realized her shift had come to an end.

"Hey Janiece," a coworker said.

She stared at the coworker.

"Why are you still here? It's past nine."

"Are you serious? Girl, let me leave before I crack up in this place." Janiece rode all the way home listening to her favorite tunes on the radio. When she pulled up into her grandparents' house, she spoke and got her daughter ready to leave.

"Your baby hasn't been feeling good today. She had a fever of 102.7 and I gave her some Motrin. You might need to take her to the doctor, 'Neece," her grandma stated as she handed the baby to her.

"Nah, I got it. Her fever will go away."

Her grandma put her hand on her curvy hips. "You won't know for sure unless you take her, Janiece."

"Listen to your Grandma now. I believe she's a lot more experienced than you," her grandpa added.

Janiece didn't appreciate them acting like she couldn't take care of her child. "Yeah, I'll do that Thursday. That's when I'm off."

"Okay. What time are you bringin' her tomorrow?"

"I'm not. Jennifer is gon' to watch her."

Grandma answered, "Oh. I don't mind watchin' my baby you know that."

"I know but I promised Jennifer that she could watch her tomorrow."

"Okay," they said together as she packed the baby bag to go. She told them that she would see them Thursday. She knew her grandma watched her as she buckled the baby in the backseat of the car.

Janiece waved her hands toward her grandparents

before starting her vehicle and pulling away.

Later Tuesday night, Janiece placed the baby in her crib and her baby started to cry loud and hard. Janiece didn't respond right away instead she lay down on the bed because she was exhausted from work. She figured she would cry herself to sleep. She felt a little bad to allow her baby to cry. She looked over toward her baby and noticed her baby right sided limbs were shaking and her eyes were rolling backward in her head. It freaked her out and she jumped up out of bed to grab her child but the quivering of her baby's limbs had stopped within a few seconds. So she laid back down. Janiece hadn't realized she had fallen asleep. She jumped up quickly and searched for her baby. She pressed her hand over her heart and realized she was in the crib next to her.

Janiece looked over in the crib and noticed that her little girl's eyes were staring up at the ceiling. She called her name but the baby didn't respond. Janiece assumed her baby was ignoring her for a minute because babies do that sometimes. She called again but no response. It scared her. She quickly reached down in the crib to pick

234

up her baby and felt her daughter's clothes were damp. Panicked rushed in. She called her baby and still no response. The only thing she could do was call 911. She told the operator what her daughter was doing. The operator asked her home address. Janiece couldn't think straight. She wondered why the operator was being slow and casual with her when this was an emergency. The operator was too slow. Janiece hung up the phone. She wrapped her daughter in a blanket and rushed to the hospital.

"Somebody help me, my daughter is unconscious," she screamed hysterically holding her baby tight in her arms.

"Ma'am, when did this happen?" a nurse asked.

"Please don't let my baby die," was all she could mutter.

A few minutes later, one of the nurses got all the information from her as she waited in the waiting room until her grandparents arrived. Her grandma and grandpa walked into the hospital around eleven o'clock that night. Her grandpa was the first one to spot her. She was bent over crying her eyes out when he placed his arms around her and held on. She couldn't look up into his eyes. She felt her grandma's presence beside her. Her grandma reached out and grabbed her hands in hers.

She heard her grandma speak, "You want me to call Jennifer?"

Janiece nodded her head. "And Shaneema."

She wondered why the doctors were taking a long time to come get her and then she heard her name. She looked up at the clock and it read one o'clock in the morning.

"Ms. Turner?"

They looked up to see a brown-skinned middle-age doctor. His eyes were low as he spoke. "I'm sorry but we tried everything."

Janiece stood up. "What does that mean?"

Her grandparents stood up alongside her and held her. The doctor once again spoke, "She's gone."

"Noooooooooo!" she screamed.

It was happening to her all over again. Someone she loved had passed away. She collapsed into her grandpa's arms and cried. She heard someone else hollering along with her and she guessed it was her grandma. Janiece didn't know how but she and her grandma were seated together holding each other. Just for a moment, she looked over her shoulder and spotted her grandpa talking to that same doctor who just delivered the most devastating news.

"Why did God take her away!" she hollered.

"Baby, you can't blame God. He has a purpose for everything he does," her grandma answered her as they waited on Grandpa to return.

The next few hours were a blur to her. She knew she wasn't there mentally. Janiece zoned out because she didn't remember when they pulled up to her grandparents' house or how she was lying down under the covers of her old bed. She couldn't remember if they kissed her goodnight or not. She lay down under the covers drained. Tears seemed to be her best friend again. *Dead, numbed, and frozen,* she knew her life would never be the same again. Her daughter was the only thing that was keeping her strong. Now she was gone. Tear after tear rolled down her face. Janiece was tired of crying and losing someone close to her. All she knew in her mind was that it was the doctor's fault. He didn't do enough to save her child. She hated them. She hated doctors.

Chapter 25

Mine eyes is consumed because of grief... Psalm 6:7.

Janiece

Days had passed since her child's funeral. The signs were there but she ignored them. She thought a little prayer and Motrin was the cure to break the fever. But the elevated temperature turned into something serious. A status epilepticus seizure. Signs of eye-rolling, stiff limbs and twitching on one side of the body. *Her daughter.* She learned that her baby died from not breathing.

Janiece was still out of it. She did not eat regularly so her grandma had to feed her because she was incapable of doing it herself. She felt like a zombie again. First her mama. Now her daughter. Janiece didn't know how long she stayed at her grandparents' house. She lost her daughter before she could start school. *School.* Her smile didn't reach its full potential. It was too much. This life. Death after death.

She heard a knock on her door. She knew it was either her grandma or grandpa. She turned her head toward the door and stared. The tears began to fill up in her eyes again. The door opened and her grandma was holding a food tray in her hand. Janiece watched her grandma saunter in the room and placed the tray on the computer desk. Usually, her grandma placed the food tray on the desk and quickly left out the room but this time she lingered. She strolled closer to her and sat on the edge of the bed.

"Sugah, I know you're sad. We're all tore up but I want you to try to eat something baby," her grandma leaned down and kissed her on the forehead. "I'll call your friends to come to see about you," her grandma said as she got up from the bed.

Janiece couldn't answer as her mind wasn't in the present. It was in the past. Loving her daughter. She watched the door close behind her grandma as she exited the room. Janiece turned her head slightly and glanced at the food before her. The aroma was captivating. A bowl of homemade macaroni and cheese and a side of collards with a piece of cornbread with a dash of ketchup on the side. She smiled slightly knowing that was the food to her heart. It was tempting but she made no move to eat.

She lay there contemplating her life at the moment. Questioning God's purpose in her life. Questioning herself. All the what ifs darkened her memories. It was hours later when she heard her door open again. This time she didn't look toward the door, she just gazed up to the ceiling.

"Ooh, do I smell macaroni in here. Girl, you're gonna let your food get cold." Jennifer's voice was annoying to her.

Janiece tilted her head to the left. She watched Jennifer saunter to the bowl, place the spoon inside the bowl and scoop up the macaroni. She then spun around and faced her. Lifting the spoon and extending it toward her, Janiece's eyes bucked wide. She mashed her lips together. And shook her head no.

"Look here now, I ain't come over here for you to tell me no." Jennifer placed the bowl on the desk and strolled toward her and lifted her by placing two pillows behind her back. She went back and grabbed the bowl.

This time Janiece opened her mouth slowly and began

eating the food Jennifer was feeding to her. After she cleared the bowl of macaroni, she tried the collards and cornbread. Another knock on the door.

"I forgot your sweet tea," her grandma announced with her eyes stretched wide. "I'll take that tray. Thank you, Jennifer. You're a blessing from God."

"You're welcome," was all Jennifer stated.

Jennifer suddenly got up and looked at her dresser. She grabbed the hair comb; brush and some Cantu leave-in conditioner. "Girl, I'm gon' to hook you up because we're gon' to get out the house for a bit."

Janiece stared at her exhaustingly. It was useless to argue with Jennifer so she let her. Janiece sat up and turned around while Jennifer did her hair and then told her that she was about to find her something to wear after she took a shower. She once again looked at a crazed Jennifer and nodded her head. Jennifer helped her get out of bed and into the shower.

Janiece was sitting on the passenger side of Jennifer's mama car as she rode the city. Her friend tried to speak words of wisdom to her but she didn't want to hear anything. Instead, she turned the radio on and let the music flow from the speakers.

Jennifer pulled up to Moe's Southwestern Grill drive thru. As she ordered their food, she pulled up to the window and paid for the meal. She saw out her peripheral view that Lyric had some girl he was hugged up with walking out of the restaurant.

"It's gon' to be okay," Jennifer said as she saw what she was looking at.

She don't know how he knew it was her sitting in the car but Lyric turned to her. He started walking toward the vehicle but stopping midway when he shouted, "I'm sorry for your loss."

Janiece quickly shot up and screamed, "I hate you!"

"Janiece, don't let him upset you. It's not about him. It's about your peace." Jennifer stated as she retrieved the food from the cashier. "Girl, don't even worry about that," she said as she sped away.

"I hate him," was all she could mutter.

When Jennifer dropped her back to her grandparents' house, she moseyed into her old bedroom. She lay atop the covers and allowed the tears to fall. Thoughts of her daughter consumed her thoughts. How was she going to make it now? Why wasn't she more attentive to her daughter's needs? Will there be more heartache and pain?

Chapter 26

For the sufferer: There's hope in hardship and comfort for endurance-Charles Stanley

Grandpa

"Janiece, it's time to get up for church," Grandpa said. It was Sunday. He figured some church would do them all some good.

Knock. Knock.

He waited for Janiece to answer him. Whether she said 'I'm up or I'm getting up' but she didn't say anything. He knocked again before opening the door. He saw the covers thrown over her head. He tiptoed toward her bed and sat on the edge.

"Baby girl, I know you don't feel like gettin' up but I would like for you to come to church with us this mornin'."

"I'm not gon'," she mumbled.

He rubbed her back. "When you're troubled in the spirit, you go to God and he will strengthen you."

"I can't," she paused briefly. "I ain't talked to God in

a minute."

"Where's your faith, Janiece?" his gentle voice asked her.

"How can I pray to God when he took my child away from me?"

He heard her mumble under the sheets. "Janiece, do you remember Job in the bible?" His voice heavily burdened by his granddaughter's words.

"Yes, sir."

"Job had everything until the devil went to God and asked if he could test him. God was sure of himself that Job was indeed a good and faithful servant. He lost his family, his livestock died, he became sickened with boils, and his friends talked about him. He had lost everything and he was saddened because of that. In the midst of his sufferings, he didn't curse God. He even wanted to die but he never sinned against God," he paused briefly. "I said that to say to you, God giveth and he taketh away. But first, you must repent, baby girl. For God tests his children/his people daily for our faith because we're set aside. What is faith, Janiece?"

"Things hoped for but ain't seen."

"God builds our faith upon trials, hardships, and tribulations. Why? Because he's building up our faith in him. We're his servants. To serve him. For he sent his son Jesus. Jesus says he's gon' to prepare a place for you. Yes, we will see our loved ones again. That place isn't on this earth but a holy place where we will serve our Lord and see our loved ones if you're His. That New Jerusalem city of gold. Baby girl, God is testing you and you need to answer your calling."

"What calling?" she asked in a whisper.

"The calling as a believer. As a believer, we are to keep the faith. To trust in his word. To seek out his will for our life. We have to stop focusing on our situation and turn to Him."

"I don't know if God wanna hear me."

It broke his heart to see his granddaughter in so much pain again. He did know why God allowed so much turmoil in this world because we 'his people' have turned from him. He began to cite 2 Chronicles 14; "If my people, which are called by my name, shall humble themselves, and pray, and seek my face, and turn from their wicked ways; then will I hear from heaven, and will forgive their sin, and will heal their land."

He continued with his lesson. "God said in Matthew 11; Come to me all who are weary and carry your burdens, and I will give you rest. Take my yoke upon you. Let me teach you, because I am humble and gentle at heart, and you will find rest for your souls," he said, getting up from Janiece's bed. He kissed her on the forehead and began to walk out of the room.

"What does that mean?" she asked.

"It means he wants you to fall on your knees and ask for forgiveness. Let God know how angry you are. Let him know that you're hurtin' and when you do all of that, you still have to give him the praise. While don' that you're not to blame God, to curse him. Get angry yes but we don't curse him."

"You hear me, 'Neece? Don't give up on God just yet. God is waitin' on you. He loves you." And with that Grandpa left the room, hoping his words of encouragement did some good to Janiece.

He walked where his wife was standing by the kitchen door.

"Where's Janiece?"

"She's stayin' in today. Let's go and ask the pastor to pray for her. She needs it. We all need it."

Chapter 27

*The Lord is close to the brokenhearted and saves
those who are crushed in the spirit. Psalm 34:18*

Janiece

Soon as her grandparents left, Janiece had the urge to
leave the house. She called Jennifer and asked her if she
could meet her at her apartment. She heard the hesitancy
in Jennifer's voice but Jennifer told her that she would be
over as soon as her mother came back from the store.
When Janiece opened her apartment door, she froze in the
doorway. Her steps were few but managed to close the
door. Her legs couldn't carry the rest of her body. It was
shortly after and within moments, it hit her. The sadness
hit her hard. She collapsed on the kitchen floor, bawling.
An hour passed before she got up from the floor. She
went and sat on the sofa and then she heard a knocking on
her door. Swinging the door opened, she caught sight of
Jennifer and spun around.

"It's gon' to be alright," Jennifer said as she threw her
arms around her.

Shrugging out of Jennifer's grasp, she untwisted herself from her embrace. She sauntered in the living room and the playpen caught her eyes. Grief hit her in the chest. Pain even smiled at her. She considered running away at the moment. She tried to block the playpen from her mind so she picked up the remote and turned on the television to 'The Parkers'. The show did nothing to distract her. Sooner than later Jennifer joined her on the sofa. The ton of grief enveloped her with a strong force. She sprang to her feet and strolled into her bedroom.

This was a critical moment in time. The crib. Her daughter's shoes. She never thought she would be one of *those* people but she snapped. She spotted a collection of little black girls' posters on the wall along with other framed art prints of little girls. She marched toward them. The tears ran down her cheeks. She raised her right hand and traced the silhouette of the little girl on the picture. And then starting at the top of the poster, she balled her fist and crumbled the poster, ripping it off the wall. She did it repeatedly until all the posters were down. She turned to the left and saw the frames next. She gripped the framed little girls and snatched them off the wall. And onto the next. She did it so forcefully that she injured her left shoulder in the process. She whimpered but it didn't stop her. It clouded her memory of what she will never get back. Her daughter was gone and it angered her. It enraged her. She saw red.

Jennifer ran into the room and yelled, "What're you don'?"

"My little girl is gone and she's not comin' back."

She glanced and paced inside the closet. Pulling the dresses off the hangers, wire hangers, and plastic hangers incited her with hatred. An empty box in the corner of the closet caught her attention. She began throwing the clothes in the box. "What's the use of havin' her clothes here when she won't be wearin' them?"

Jennifer stood frozen inside her room, shocked. "What if you have another girl? You could save them for her."

Janiece's dark, tear-stained eyes shot daggers at her. "You want me to erase her like that!"

"No, I didn't mean it like that."

"Well! Come over here and help me get rid of them before I lose it!" shouted Janiece as she looked around her small bedroom apartment.

"I think you should save this one just in case," Jennifer announced as she pulled a Metallic Floral Jacquard dress and bloomers set from the box.

With anger and sadness in her eyes, Janiece snatched the dress out of Jennifer's hands and tossed the dress back in the box.

"Never mind, I got this," Janiece said as she paced around her bedroom. "Can you at least get rid of that crib? Oh, the playpen too. Thanks!"

"Yeah, I could take it to the Salvation Army."

"Whatever," was all she said.

She heard the pitter-patter of Jennifer's footsteps leave the room. Minutes later, she heard Jennifer calling her but she ignored her. Instead, she yelled, "Go ahead and take it. I'll holla at you later."

The sound of the front door squeaking as it was being shut, Janiece walked out to see. Her eyes narrowed at the non-existent baby furniture in her living room. Sweat formed onto her forehead as she overworked herself. In an instant, she fell over the couch and wailed like a newborn baby.

Her heart began racing. She needed space. She knew she couldn't go back to her grandparents' tonight. She didn't think to call them at this moment either. She felt a pressure building up in her head. She was tired of crying. It seemed as if they were made just for her. Her reality came crashing down. Bang! Clack! Boom! Wham! Poof! Her heart ached. She couldn't breathe.

Later on Sunday night, she received a text from Jennifer.

Jennifer: *Hey, your grandparents were scared that you weren't home when they return from church and so they called me. I told them I helped you get rid of some stuff today and that you were going to call them tomorrow to let them know how you feel. But your grandpa insisted he was going to pay you a visit in the morning.*

Janiece smiled. She felt bad in how she asked Jennifer to help her but she went ballistic when she offered to help

254

her. She hoped Jennifer could forgive her. She was truly sorry for her outburst. She just was troubled at the moment. She sent Jennifer a text back.

Janiece: *Thank you so much and I'm sorry I acted out the norm today. You were only helpin'. Thanks again. But I'll give my grandpa a call tonight.*

Janiece called the house number but her grandpa answered the phone. She told him that she needed some time alone and she was going to be okay. She assured him that she would visit tomorrow if he didn't beat her first.

It was around midnight when Janiece packed up the two boxes of her daughter's clothes, shoes, toys, and blankets. She placed the boxes in the stroller since she didn't feel like driving. She left on foot to throw the boxes in the dumpster not far from her apartment. When she set the boxes on the ground, she lifted one box and threw it between the slit in the dumpster. Then the other box. Leaving the stroller there too. Before walking away, tears silently fell down her face.

"I'm sorry baby girl. Know that mommy loves you and will continue to love you. I won't ever forget about you or try to replace you. You are my heart. Love you, beautiful baby girl," she said as she blew a kiss into the air.

Janiece walked away from the dumpster. She did not feel like going back to her apartment so she just wandered. She strolled and marched until she came upon a bridge. The bridge wasn't that deep. It probably had about six feet of water in it. If the sane Janiece was thinking, she would have told this Janiece not to stand too close. She shrugged her shoulders. Stared ahead into the night. Thousands of memories flashed across her mind but none of that mattered now. *Voices.* The voices, she heard inside of her head told her that she killed her baby. And they kept repeating it. Janiece tried to fight back but she lost when the tears clouded her vision. More voices, she heard. But this time it seemed like they were getting closer to her. She finally erupted, "I killed her."

Yes, the voices won. She had admitted that she killed her baby and now she didn't deserve to live either.

"I killed her," she cried. *First, her mother and now her baby. Why?* Soon as she was about to ask God to forgive her, she heard another voice close up and personal.

Chapter 28

Have mercy upon me, O Lord, for I am weak, O Lord, heal me...Psalms 6:2.

Josiah

Josiah, a determined medical student, was working his third night in the emergency department. A fifty-four-year-old male arrived at the emergency room after experiencing a heart attack. They quickly took the man straight for an invasive procedure. They performed a left heart catheterization. The procedure consisted of a catheter inserted through a peripheral vessel in the arm or the groin which test the blood flow and they found blockages. They had to insert three stents in his arteries. Usually, the procedure is successful with experienced physicians and deaths from a diagnostic procedure are low. But this man started bleeding profusely during the procedure. The team of doctors used every source of knowledge to stop the bleeding but nothing was working.

Code blue. Code blue.

That code meant someone has decoded or died. The

complications that persisted on this man was that he had another heart attack on top of a stroke. It was nothing he nor the other doctors could do to save the patient. He felt like a failure. He didn't come into this field to lose people but to try his best to save them. *He knew everyone was meant to die but why this night,* he pondered. After scrubbing off the blood and removing them and changed into his regular clothes, he took a long walk to clear his mind. This night weighed heavily on his heart. Thank God it was his last case for the night. Was he really ready for the cardiology field? He strode out the hospital along the corridor of the sidewalk and around the corner. He couldn't stop walking now. He kept strolling and found himself a few feet from a small bridge. He was in his own thoughts until something caught his attention. A shadowy figure jerked. He couldn't believe what he saw with his eyes. He saw a woman standing on the edge of the small bridge. He kept walking but didn't want to scare her. As he got closer to the bridge, he glanced down at his watch. It read 12:30 a.m. The figure jerked again. His mind told him to run. And he did. When he got to the edge of the bridge, he heard the woman yelling, '*I killed her*'. Who she killed didn't matter at the moment. What he wanted to do was talk some sense into her. As he approached her, she turned to stare at him with tear-stained eyes.

"Ma'am, you don't want to do this. It's not worth it. Whatever your problem is, it can be fixed. God can fix anything," he pleaded.

"God can't fix it."

Stunned by her words, he announced as he crept toward her. "Nothing is impossible with God."

She stood there in silence as he continued his plea. The more he tried talking to her, the more agitated she became. She turned back toward the water. Without warning, he grabbed her and wrestled her to the ground. Elbowing him in the jaw, he straddled his legs around her until she stopped fighting him. Once calm, he jumped to his feet.

Before standing her up, she cried out, "I killed her, I killed her."

"Why did she leave me? I was gonna take her to the doctor but it was too late. She gone," she stated as she wept into his arms.

Josiah bowed his head and said a quick prayer to God. He led the woman to his car not far from the hospital. He opened the passenger door, sat her on the inside while he walked around and got in on the driver's side. As he drove his car, he kept asking her where she lived. No words escaped her mouth so he was stuck with her for the night. He knew he had a good heart. Since he couldn't help his patient, he figured he could help this distraught woman somehow. He asked the woman her address again and still no reply. Just the silent tears. He figured he would let her sleep off her anger at his home. He put her into his spare bedroom. When Josiah left for work the next morning, he hoped the young woman found her way out of his house.

Janiece

Hours later, Janiece woke up to music playing somewhere in the house. She peeked out of the cover and glanced around. She didn't recognize any of it. *I've been kidnapped again,* she thought. Hearing voices outside her door, Janiece immediately looked under the comforter set and saw that she still had on the same clothes from last night. Last night was blurry but she remembered. A mistake she was going to make. Tears escaped from her eyes. As she got up, the door opened and there stood a man. *Dang, he looks like Morris Chestnut but two shades lighter with a reddish-brown undertone.* He was medium built. He had a bald head and a small goatee. He had dark brown slanted eyes, a heart-shaped nose, and kissable lips. He paused in the door sporting a wife-beater and blue basketball shorts.

"Who are you?" she jumped up frantically, looking around the room for something, anything. She looked around the room and saw an umbrella lying in the corner. She quickly grabbed it and jumped on top of the bed.

"Whoa," he said as he threw his hands up in the air. "I

didn't expect you to still be here."

"What do you mean? Why did you kidnap me?" she asked.

She saw him raise his eyebrows while holding his hands in the air. "Ma'am, you are free to leave. Just put down the umbrella and get off my bed."

Still pointing the umbrella at him with the sharp end, she eased down off the bed. "Back up," she ordered.

She regarded him as he backed up into the hallway. She sidestepped him and stood in front of him. As they entered the living room, he motioned for her to leave through the front door. She didn't follow his direction pointing toward the door. She backed up into the kitchen.

"Uh, the front door is this way," he pointed to his left.

Her stomach growled. "I'm hungry."

"Fine, have it your way."

When she emerged from the kitchen, she had a sandwich in her left hand and the umbrella in her right. To her amazement, this guy carried on to his regularly scheduled program like she wasn't intruding. "How can you watch TV when you have a stranger in your house?"

she asked dumbfounded.

"I know you're not dangerous."

"Oh really? Why did you save me last night then?"

He turned to her. "Do you remember that?"

"Yeah, I wasn't drunk or anything."

Amused, he sarcastically replied. "Well, it would have been better if you were. No person in their right mind would have done what you tried to do last night."

She screamed, "You wouldn't know!" she stated after throwing the umbrella on the floor while still holding onto the sandwich.

He sprang to his feet. "Know what?" he asked as he lunged for her.

"Don't touch me!" she hollered as panicking tears seeped out her eyes. She placed the sandwich on the table before walking toward the door.

The man stood there staring back at her. "What is wrong with you?"

"I killed her," she sobbed putting her hands up to her face to cover up the tears she didn't want this strange man to see. She was hurting all over again. This man. This man was annoying.

He asked if he could come closer and only hold her and nothing more. She nodded because she needed someone to care for. Yet she didn't feel scared or nervous to be in his house or his arms. She noticed how he held his hands in the air as he tiptoed toward her. He dropped his hands and wrapped his strong arms around her and spoke softly in her ears.

"Who did you kill?" he asked somberly.

His scent immediately permeated her nose. He smelled of a warm, vanilla musk scent. She lifted her nose further into his shoulder and whispered, "I can't tell you."

"Well, whenever you feel like it, I'm all ears," he stated.

"Can I spend another night, please?"

"What's your name?"

"Janiece," was all she replied.

Chapter 29

Lead me O Lord, in thy righteousness because of mine enemies; make thy way straight before my face Psalm 5:8.

Janiece

She awakened Tuesday morning and began walking the green mile home to her apartment. When she entered her apartment, she collapsed and fell asleep on the sofa. Hours passed before waking up to the ringing of her cell phone.

"Hello," she answered groggily.

"Where the hell are you?" the man hollered.

"Who is this?"

"Your Grandpa!"

She answered in a croaky voice, "Oh, I'm at home."

"When did you get back, 'Neece? Because you weren't there last night when we came lookin' for you. You ain't back in dem streets, are you?"

She chuckled.

"Why are you laughin'? Are you high or something?"

Wishing she was high on something the way she acted the night before. "No Grandpa. I just went out to get some fresh air. I'm good. I got my head in order now."

"Okay 'cause you had me and your grandma worried 'bout you. We don't want you to do anything foolish because we know you're gon' through a tough time. I mean we all are," he declared. "Well baby girl, we want you to get your rest and then come visit us when you're ready," he paused, "I love you."

"Love you too grandpa. I'm sorry I'm takin' y'all through so much."

"That's true but we forgive you. You just have to learn to forgive yourself."

"Yes, sir. I'm gon' to ask Jennifer and Shaneema to come over later."

"Alright baby. We want to see you soon," her grandpa uttered.

"Yes, sir. Goodnight."

It was hours later when she hit up her two best friends to come over. Like true friends, they were over in thirty minutes with snacks. They sat on the sofa and she watched how Shaneema looked around but didn't part her mouth to ask her where her daughter's stuff was. She was happy to have them apart of her life especially bringing snacks because she knew they were going to have 'girl talk' tonight. Janiece muted the TV and looked at her friends.

"I have a confession," she said crossing her legs, sitting Indian style on the sofa.

"What?" they said in unison.

"What I'm about to say is gon' to sound crazy. I know I shouldn't have but I did and I don't want y'all to judge me either. Promise?" she asked.

"This shit sounds serious, hold on let me grab a bowl to put this popcorn in. Ya'll want a soda?" Shaneema asked getting up from the sofa and walking into the kitchen.

When Shaneema reentered the living room, she poured the popcorn in the bowl and passed out two sodas. She also grabbed the bag of peanut M&Ms. "Go ahead. I'm ready now."

Janiece chuckled slightly. "Remember not to judge because I know *you,* Jennifer."

"She good, go ahead Janiece," Shaneema exclaimed grabbing a handful of M&Ms.

"I ain't promising you that. But I ain't gonna judge 'cause we all have done some crazy things in our lifetime. So what did you do?" asked Jennifer.

"First, I want to say I'm sorry Jennifer for the way I treated you Sunday night."

"You're forgiven."

"Thanks, girl, I needed to hear that," was all Janiece said.

"Girl, you know you still my girl although we fight."

"So what you do?" Shaneema asked cutting off their conversation.

"Well y'all already know what I've been through before in my lifetime but I think this is the worst of them all."

"I don't know about that. What about when you were—you know?" asked Shaneema.

Janiece cut her eyes at her. "Worst then that," Janiece

said solemnly. "You know how you have suicidal thoughts at times."

"Yeah and no," they said.

"Well around twelve that night Jennifer, I gathered those two boxes and walked to the dumpster and threw them away. After crying for my daughter, I didn't feel like gon' home so I ended up on the Paramount Bridge."

"Okay, what's wrong with that?" she asked dumbfounded.

Shaneema hollered. "Girl, she thought about jumping off the bridge, that's what."

Jennifer quickly covered her mouth and looked at her for a long time and then glanced away.

"I know and I was completely out of my mind. I heard voices that said I killed my baby. And next thing I know a guy pulled me from the bridge. After that, I woke up at his house."

"What you mean you woke up at his house?" Jennifer asked suspiciously.

"Just what I said."

"He ain't try nothin' wit you, did he?"

"No, and that's the good part." Janiece shivered underneath their gazes. "I mean I wasn't scared to be left alone with him either. It was like God was watchin' over me or something. I don't know. I'm just talkin' crazy. I just had this feeling."

"Damn Janiece, we did some crazy things in life but I ain't never thought nothin' like that." Shaneema leaned forward, holding the M&M's in her hands. "Why would you want to do something as crazy as kill yourself because your baby didn't make it?" she asked, her voice accusing as she squinted her eyes.

Janiece yelled, "That's the point. My baby is *dead*. How am I supposed to survive?"

"Girl, the only way to survive is through Jesus. What did he say? He said to give all your burdens to him and he will comfort you. Although we experience hardship in our lives, he still wants us to give him praise through it all. I remember this saying, 'If he brings you to it, he will bring you through it.'"

"Amen," Jennifer uttered, grabbing Janiece's and Shaneema's hand. "I think we should pray."

"Our Father who art in heaven, we come to you today asking for forgiveness on Janiece's sake. Father, she's trouble in the spirit and needs your protection and guidance as she figures out her purpose on earth. We ask that you give her strength to overcome her struggle with depression. We know depression is real but Father you're stronger than any problems we face. You are the Father, the one who loves us when we repent and come to you. Lord, she thought that she had the say but Father you send your angels when we need them the most. Lord when we don't understand why things happen to us, we know that you have a reason for everything you do. Again Lord, for you say, 'We pick our paths but you direct them, Lord.' Father, I ask of you that you bring comfort in her life because she needs you, Lord. Father, please forgive her for her sin and ours as we live in this journey of life. For you said, 'ask and it will be given, seek and we shall find, knock and the door will be open.' Thank you, Father, thank you, Jesus, that you died for our sins that we may live again. In your name, Jesus. In Jesus' name, amen."

"Amen," Janiece and Shaneema muttered with tears streaming down their faces.

"Yes, that was a powerful prayer. I didn't know you could pray like that," Shaneema joked.

"Me either until a time was needed," Jennifer answered hugging her girls in a tight hug.

"I know that's right."

Shaneema placed her right hand onto Janiece's left shoulder and said, "You know you didn't kill your baby, right?"

Janiece did not respond. She closed her tear-stained eyes.

"Girl, you had no way of knowin' your baby had a status epilepticus seizure. It was God's way of getting your attention."

"By letting my baby die?" she asked bewilderedly.

Jennifer chimed in. "Girl no! God has a lot of ways bringin' our attention back to him. He does many things when we step out of the kingdom of God. You know the sayin' all things happen for a reason?"

"Yeah."

"Well when we get too caught up in ourselves, God has a way of letting us know who's in charge. God loves you and your baby girl. God is a jealous God and he just wants his children to worship him. Not to be caught up in this world. It says in Romans twelve, verse two:

'Do not be conformed to this world but be transformed by the renewing of your mind. Then you will be able to test and approve what God's will is—his good and perfect will.'

"And what does that mean Pastor Gonzalez," Janiece asked sarcastically.

"Well, it means He doesn't want you to do the same thing that everybody else does. Just because this person does nothing all day and that person smokes weed don't mean you need to do the same thing. We're set aside because we are His children. Certain things we shouldn't do because we are His. Instead, he would want you to imitate those who are of faith and wait on him so you can inherit what has been promised to you. We're here for God's purpose. He tests us each and every day. Why? I can't tell you all that because I'm not God. We as His children should return unto him and he will grant our will. You get it a lil'?"

She sniffed. "Kinda like how I used to live with Mya?"

"Correct but enough of this talk. Janiece, we love you too much for you to kill yourself over something you had no control over. God loves you too much for you to give yourself to the devil. Those voices you heard were from the devil. He rejoices when we turn away from God. If you would have taken your life, the devil would be laughing and saying you're on your way to meet him in the fire of hell. You just have to wait on the Lord."

"I hear ya girl. Thank y'all so much for believin' in me and lovin' me."

"Girl, you know we got chu'," Jennifer responded joyfully.

"And know that your grandparents love you even more and so does God," Shaneema said.

"Okay, I hear what y'all are sayin'. I'm gon' to see them tomorrow."

"Just for the record Janiece," Jennifer voiced. "I'm

stayin' wit you for a while until I know that you're back. So follow me back to mi Madre's house so I can drop off her car.

"You know I only have one bed."

"What does that mean? You ain't getting rid of me until I say so. So let's go so I can pack some of my clothes," she declared as Janiece locked up her apartment as they headed out. They hugged Shaneema and told her they will catch up later.

Chapter 30

For some who have done this have entertained angels without realizing it! Hebrews 13:2.

Janiece

It was Thursday and Janiece wanted to redecorate her apartment. They went to Walmart and got separated when Jennifer walked down another aisle.

Ring. Ring.

"Girl, where you at?" Jennifer asked.

"In the aisle with the floral decorations with the fake flowers."

"What aisle is that?"

"I don't know," Janiece said as she turned around and looked up toward the signage. "It's aisle seven."

"Oh, I know where that is. Mi Madre loves some candles," Jennifer replied as she hung up the phone.

Jennifer stood in front of her and asked, "You redecoratin'?"

"Yeah," was all she said before picking up a tricolor vase and two Fern plants and placing them into the buggy. As they continued to walk down the aisle, a familiar person waved. *Did he just wave at me? Oh, shoot, that's him*, she spoke. In a rush, Janiece pushed the buggy to the next aisle.

"Girl, what's wrong wit you now?"

"That's him."

"Him who?" Jennifer questioned as she twisted around.

Janiece tugged her arm. "Don't turn around. He might come."

"Who're you talkin' about for I bust you out?"

"The one I ended up at his house. The angel as y'all likes to call it." Janiece blew out a long breath.

"For real? Where he at? I gotta take a look at him."

"Don't do that!" Janiece shouted.

Janiece tried to play it off as she watched the man standing by a woman who seemed to be his mother because of her appearance. She pulled on Jennifer's arm to get her to go the other way but her bighead left her alone with the buggy.

"Jennifer. Jennifer," she called out but the man was

looking directly at her. She turned her head back toward the decorations.

"Yeah," Jennifer answered her. "Over here."

Janiece jerked the buggy fast around the corner and crashed into another cart. "Oh I'm sorry," she announced apologetically, looking up into two pairs of eyes looking at her.

"It's okay," he said, his voice low.

"Oops, sorry my girl can be clumsy sometimes," Jennifer chuckled. "I'm Jennifer. It's nice to meet you," she stuck her hand out.

"Oh hi, I'm Josiah and this is my mother," he looked at her then Jennifer. "It's nice to meet you, Jennifer."

"Hi ma'am," Jennifer spoke, stepping beside Janiece.

Janiece watched how his mother spoke kindly to them and lifted her brows toward Jennifer to signal her to walk off and leave them. Janiece called Jennifer's name but she and the woman just left them standing there.

"Mama," was all Josiah said as he glanced at her.

"We meet again huh?" Janiece spoke hesitantly while looking everywhere but at him. She couldn't stand to look into his piercing eyes.

He asked in a stern tone. "What'd you do with your hair?"

Janiece cocked her neck to the side. "What, you don't like my hair?"

"I hope you were in your right mind when you cut it," he verbalized with a straight face.

Janiece thought her layered cut hairstyle with golden highlights was cute. When she wanted to start anew with her life, she felt a new hairstyle would be the first thing she changed about herself.

"I hope you're in your right mind for askin' me that. If you don't mind, I have to go," she said as she pushed the buggy away from his and pulled out her cell phone and called Jennifer. She told Jennifer to meet her in checkout line seven. She didn't even check to see if he was still in the same spot.

"Girl, what'd he say? 'Cause his mama had plenty to say." Jennifer professed as she stood beside her in line.

Pulling out her Visa debit card to pay for her items, Janiece answered. "Girl, he had the nerve to ask me what

I did to my hair. I basically told him to bounce."

Jennifer laughed.

"What I'm for real."

"I bet you are. If you don't want to get with that then I do. What's his number?" asked Jennifer, laughing.

"Did you not just hear me? I told him to bounce."

Jennifer pushed Janiece on the shoulders playfully. "Girl, whatever. What happened to the old Janiece?"

Janiece smiled as she sang, "Dead and gone."

They laughed as they walked out of Wal-Mart to Janiece's car. Pulling out the parking spot, Janiece gazed at Jennifer and asked her what his mama had to say. Jennifer chuckled and basically told her that her son is a good man and she wants grandchildren. Janiece said nothing. When they got back to the apartment, Janiece turned on the radio to block out what happened at Wal-Mart today. Jennifer was in the kitchen making tacos for dinner. They danced to the old jam *Hoochie Mama* by 2 Live Crew.

Chapter 31

As soon as I pray, you answer me; you encourage me by giving me strength. Psalm 138:3.

Josiah

After he ran into Janiece that day in Walmart, he couldn't shake her off. Small thoughts made his heart pitter-patter. Somehow she snaked herself into his life. Whether it was by accident or God. *Was it God?* He didn't know if it was God himself but their chance encounter had him spooked. He thought about that day ever since meeting her.

For a moment, maybe it was a figment of his imagination. Maybe she wasn't real. Maybe God was testing him? He had so many questions for God. Why was she placed in his life now? Why did their interaction cause a stir in the lower part of his abdomen? Why did it take for him to lose a patient to help someone else's dilemma? What was God saying to him?

He shook his head. Just the other day, he recalled telling his mama that he wasn't ready for a relationship.

When he saw her in the store, her appearance shocked him. She was gorgeous. He didn't know why he said what he said but he did. He chuckled recalling her response. Her shoulder-length hairstyle intrigued him. She looked sophisticated. He guessed she was supposed to look oppressed or something but not what she appeared to be.

As he parked his car in front of his mama's house, an inkling feeling came over him. He wanted to be around her. Smell her hair. Hear her laughter. See her eyes twinkle. Feel how smooth her skin felt. See her smile. See if her freckles darkened under the rays of the sun. Anything just to be near he would give.

He entered his mama's house for a quick visit. He kissed his mama on the cheek and he spent the next hour there. He left her house and drove home. When he got home, he switched on the radio. He turned it to some Techno. *'Better Off Alone'* was playing. He listened to this type of music when he wanted to distract himself from outside interference such as Janiece. His stomach growled suddenly realizing he hasn't had any solid food all day.

Any other time he would have enjoyed a quiet night at home but he couldn't sit still to calm his crazy thoughts. His mind ran overtime. He hopped up, grabbed his keys, and found his self-parked at Moe's Southwestern Grill. Since the weather was nice in the latter of July around eight o'clock at night, he stepped inside the restaurant. He stood in the assembly line and let the staff make him a 'Wrong Doug', a wrap Served with chicken, beans, shredded cheese, pico de gallo and Moe's Famous Queso, stacked between two crunchy corn shells wrapped in a grilled tortilla. Not that God had anything to do with timing which he did but the young woman and her friend walked inside of the restaurant.

The corner of his mouth curved higher when they went to the assembly line and ordered 'Earmuffs' bowls with seasoned rice, beans, shredded cheese, pico de gallo and chicken. His eyes followed them as they sauntered to the drink station. His mouth bent noticing that Janiece was like into mixing all of her sodas together.

He stared awkwardly as they found a table a few feet away from him. Janiece sat with her back facing him and

Jennifer sat facing him. He waved and watched Jennifer's eyes stretch wide. He watched the interaction between Janiece and Jennifer. He wondered would she turn around and waved too. But unfortunately, she didn't. He watched their every move. For some reason, the song by Tyrese *'Falling in Love'* played in his head. He didn't know what kind of mess he was in but he was falling. *Falling hard.*

Just then he thought of an idea. He sprang to his feet and placed his empty wrapper in the trash. He grabbed a napkin and asked the cashier for a pen. He scribbled on the napkin and then handed the cashier back her pen. As he marched neared their table, his heart skipped a beat. *Why the hell am I getting nervous?*

He stopped inches in front of their table. "Hello, ladies," was all he said before placing the napkin onto their table and turning around to refill his cup.

Josiah*: I would like to get to know you on a personal level.*

He saw her neck lift and figured she was laughing. She glanced over her shoulder and straight into his dark, piercing eyes. He smiled and observed as she took out a pen and wrote a message, he assumed. As they began gathering their trash, she stood up and his manhood hardened when she got up from the table, exposing her long legs under a halter top dress. Janiece strutted in his direction. She stopped inches in front of him and pushed the napkin in his hand. She didn't wear a smile. Janiece rolled her eyes instead and strutted away. He looked down and read the note. The smile he wore slowly faded away.

Janiece: *I don't want to get to know you on a personal or professional level.*

Well damn! He stomped outside after the women. He looked towards the right. He didn't see her. He glanced left. He saw her and her friend get into a red Honda. He didn't know why his heartbeat so erratically or why sweat formed upon his forehead. It was as if he just ran a mile.

"Hello, ladies."

"What the hell? Are you followin' me?" she asked as she spun around to face him.

"Uh," he was at a loss for words. He didn't know that

she would respond this way. "No, I'm sorry."

"You'd better be. If I catch you followin' me again, I'm gonna call the cops. You want me to do that?"

He shook his head.

"I didn't think so," she said. "Well, we have to be on our way. Don't let me look through my rearview mirror and catch you followin' me. Ya heard me?" she laughed as she opened and shut the door.

How he pictured getting to know her in his mind didn't quite match up physically. He felt like a dummy. *Was he chasing her?* He stared ahead at them. Just then Jennifer winked at him and then dropped a napkin on the ground. His eyes zoomed in on the brake lights until they disappeared. He strode toward the napkin and glanced down at it. To his amazement, it had writing on it. He bent down and picked it up. Seven digits. The corner of his mouth lifted. Surely it had Janiece's number on it. Jennifer was on his side. He laughed as he walked toward his car, whistling a happy tune.

When he returned home, he went straight to bed. He glanced at his answering machine. He hit play. His brother Joshua asked him where he was because they had stopped by and to call him whenever he makes it in. Since he was off tomorrow, he was going to do some cleaning. He inherited that from his mama. Whenever his mama was upset or frustrated about something, she would clean the house.

Soon as Josiah started cleaning the bathrooms in the house, he ran out of cleaning supplies. He rushed off to Family Dollar. He walked down the aisle and found Pine-Sol and Clorox. He reached across as a woman pass by. He inhaled the fruity scent and sneezed, causing the woman to glance back at him.

"Hey stranger, I promise I'm not followin' you," he said.

It was Janiece.

"Really?" she asked, placing her hand on her hips.

His eyes followed her hands onto her slim hips before glancing up into her face. "I think we found something in common."

"What's that?"

He held up the cleaning supplies.

"Yeah, my grandma always said that Saturday's was the cleanup day."

"Great minds think alike," was all he said before she left him standing there.

He listened to her mild-mannered speech as she spoke with the cashier. He paid for his items and exited the store.

She spun around holding her bags in her hand. "Do you want something? A reward for savin' my life? Well, I'm sorry I can't give you that. Now leave me alone."

Holding the two bags in his right hand, he asked, "Can I get to know you spiritually?"

Her eyes stretched wide and her head twisted. She blew out a long sigh before stalking closer to him. She pulled out a pen from her purse and wrote her number on the inside of his right palm. "Call me anytime."

With a bewildered expression, Josiah gladly accepted the number and walked to his car. There he sat pondering the scenario before pulling off from the parking lot with her number in his hand. He didn't dare let her know that he already had her number.

Chapter 32

All glory to God, who is able, through his mighty power at work within us, to accomplish infinitely more than we might ask or think. Ephesians 3:20.

Janiece

She couldn't believe it had been a month since she started to talk to Josiah after she gave him her number in the parking lot of Family Dollar. He invited her over for dinner. After admiring his love of African masks, paintings, and his one-story ranch home, he cooked dinner. When he finished cleaning up the kitchen, she observed Josiah step into the back room. She became nervous all of a sudden. She got up and sat on the sofa, waiting for his arrival. Just then she heard his heavy footsteps across the hardwood floor. She glanced back and saw he was carrying a Bible.

Oh no he didn't! What does he take me for? Does he still think I'm suicidal? How many times do I have to tell him that I'm in my right mind? I think this is where this ends, she thought. "What do you think you're doin'?" she questioned as he sat down in front of her. She didn't give him time to respond. "Oh now, you're gonna minister to me? Did you forget to tell me that you minister on the side?" she asked.

Blood rushed to her brain. She'd had enough. She sprang to her feet but before she could move, Josiah grabbed her by the arm.

"I have something to share with you."

She answered in a sarcastic tone. "What, words of wisdom? I don't need that. I've heard enough of it."

"I think you can be a witness for someone else," he stated.

"What're you talkin' about?"

"Did you forgive him?" he asked, glaring at her.

"Forgive who?" she asked as she sat down on the sofa. *The dinner had gone smoothly and now he wants to get all preachy on me. I should have known something was up with this meeting,* she thought.

"The man who has caused you grief."

"There ain't no man in my life. How many times do I have to tell you that?" she spat. *He couldn't be talking about that night, could he?*

"Why are you so bitter then?" he barked, letting her arm go.

"See this is why I gotta leave," she waved her hands in the air. "You don't know me."

"But I want to know you." His voice was muffled.

"Why? So you can throw it in my face later on? No, I don't need it or you."

"Who did you kill?"

Janiece stopped dead in her tracks. She dropped her head. Without turning around, the tears began to fall. She didn't want to start crying again but certain stuff rang dear to her heart. She had her back toward him when she felt his strong arms hug her from the back. She stood there with her hands over her face and cried silently.

"My little girl. I killed her. I didn't mean to. They said they couldn't do anything to help her. She was gone."

He asked carefully and remorseful, "Who couldn't help her?"

"The doctors. I brought her in but it was too late. My little girl, she's gone and I can't bring her back. She'd...

died of a seizure but I didn't know. It was too late," was all she could utter.

"I know it's hard but God has a plan for everything he does. God cares for his children," she heard him say as he stood in front of her now. He allowed her to cry in his arms again. He slid her hands down from her face and whispered sweet nothings in her ear.

"I'd like to talk if you don't mind. Can you come back and sit on the sofa?" he asked with a sincere heart.

Janiece nodded her head. She allowed him to take her back to his sofa and sit her down. He then handed her some tissues and gave her a bottle of water.

"Thank you," was all she could mutter at this point.

After she finished crying, she told him about that night that led up to her standing on the bridge. He listened without interrupting her and she felt relieved.

"Have you forgiven your baby daddy?"

Her eyes shot up in pure anger. "No! Because he wanted no part of our life and I hate him for that."

He held her hand in his. "Baby girl," he said genuinely. "You have hardened your heart. Forgiveness is not for that person. It's for your own health. Forgiveness is something that takes place between the one who has been hurt and God. Have you spoken to God lately?"

She shook her head but told him that her friends went to God in prayer for her. She glanced up and regarded his sympathetic expression as he stared back into her sad eyes. His calling her baby girl brought out a smile because no one else called her by that name except her grandpa. She also told him that she was in school for nursing soon after losing her daughter. She told him that her main focus at the moment was to turn back to God.

"I can relate because at times I felt like giving up myself. I'm so sorry that this has happened to you early in life."

She chuckled because that's all she knew. "If you think that's something, you shoulda seen me tryin' to get my mama off drugs. I was so young when she left me at my grandparents' house. You would think she would have tried to seek me but I guess she didn't love me enough."

All he could say was, "I'm sorry."

"My mama died of an overdose when I was seventeen. I went ballistic. I ran away from home."

"You were… homeless," he stammered his words.

"No, I stayed with a friend and her boyfriend. Man, did I have it good at home? But there was too much gon' on at home I didn't like. My grandma was constantly down my back so I left and regret that I left home. You know how folks say, 'you got it made at home.' I sure did. It was heaven at home and hell in the streets," she said as fresh tears cascaded down her cheeks the second time that night. "I don't know why I'm tellin' you all of this 'cause I know I'm gon' to hear it again."

He cut her off by grabbing her hands. "No, you won't. I want to be your friend. Everyone needs to vent every now and then."

"That's true. I guess that's what I'm don'. You're gonna think bad of me after I tell you this. Maybe I shouldn't say anything."

He quickly reassured her by rubbing his thumbs across her hands.

"The guy I hooked up with had me sellin' his drugs.

Had me standin' on the corner like an idiot," she laughed. "Not sellin' my body but sellin' his drugs while he rewarded me with shopping. Of course, it didn't bother me at the time but as I look back over my life, I can say I was really foolish. Now since I'm twenty-three, I can say I did a lot of stupid things."

"We do a lot of foolish things when we are young," he commented.

She didn't know what he meant by that. He was an angel. What could he have done?

"Anyways, he had a gig for me. Since I can sing, he had me stand on the corner to get paid. I sang whole songs for fifty, half of the song for twenty-five, and recited poetry for ten."

Now it was Josiah's turn to laugh. She quickly filled him in on the later part of her life except for the rape.

"Although you have experienced the worse part of your life, God hasn't forgotten about you. He was testin' you to see if you're strong enough to be his soldier. God needs strong believers in him. He needs to know we love him. When we turn our backs to him, God doesn't turn his back from us. He may hide every now and then but he doesn't leave. When God stands back, he's waiting for you. So Janiece God is waiting for you to give your life to him so he can turn the bad, the ugly to his goodness."

"Yeah, I know. I've come to realize that I need to rededicate my life to Christ," she saw the hesitation in his eyebrows. "I've been in the church all my life."

"Really?" he questioned. "I'm sorry but I'm just shocked to hear you say that. I thought you didn't know anything about God."

"I know, right?" she nodded her head. "Yeah, I'm a lost sheep tryin' to find my way back. And just to think, you had already judged me. What does it say? Well, it says something like 'Judge and be not judge,'" she rephrased the quote from Matthew chapter seven verse one, "I believe so don't quote me."

Flabbergasted, Josiah leaned back into the sofa.

"Well, can you pick your jaw up from the floor?" she laughed wholeheartedly.

She looked down at her watch. It was late. Time does fly when you least expect it as she started to rise.

She was shocked when he offered his spare bedroom. But she politely declined, saying, "I'm sorry but I don't know you that well. And before you say anything, I was distraught that night. That's why I stayed. Sorry I have to get gon'."

"I understand. Can I drive you home?"

"I drove, remember?"

"Oh yeah, but I don't think you should drive after tonight."

"I'm good," she said heading towards the front door. "By the way, I love your house."

"Thank you," he scratched his head. "Does the friendship still stand as an offer?"

"I don't know. You're too serious to be a friend of mine. My friends usually laugh at my corny jokes and are not stuck up."

He laughed. "You think I'm stuck up?"

"Look at you, you're soon to be a doctor in the next several months. Most doctors are stuck up."

"But I'm not. I'm down to earth."

"If you say so," she said as she tilted her head back to

laugh one more time.

"Can I at least follow you home to make sure you get there safe?"

Janiece thought it was odd but she said okay. He followed her home to the nicer apartments on the east side of LaGrange. When she pulled into her parking spot, he pulled up beside her in the empty space. When she got out, he got out.

I hope he is not expecting anything, Janiece panicked. "Uh, good night."

"Can I come up for coffee?" he asked putting it out there.

Janiece frowned. *Not him too. Why couldn't he be any different? Friends, remember that is what you asked for.*

"Uh, I don't want to bring anybody up, my friend doesn't like that," she lied knowing Jennifer did not mind if it was *him.*

"Oh, your male friend?"

"No, my girlfriend," she replied as she left him standing by his car. When she entered her apartment, she was amazed that he was still waiting on the outside when she looked out her window.

Chapter 33

Forgetting the past and looking forward to what lies ahead...for which God, through Christ Jesus, is calling us. Philippians 3:13-14.

Janiece

The next time they met up was at his house for their therapy session as Janiece called it. She sauntered inside his house. She heard soft melodies flow throughout the house. Then she heard a voice. It was gospel. *Is he gonna sanctify my soul by playing gospel?*

When he came out of the kitchen and faced her, he commented. "I know you're thinking, why is he playin' that music?"

"It ran across my mind," she said as she sat down on the sofa.

"I think well when I hear gospel."

"Don't we all," she joked with her arms crossed. "Why am I even here?"

"Because you need to vent."

"I can do that at home. I don't need you. And who

said you were certified? I thought you were a medical student as in future M.D., not P.H.D."

"I am."

She twisted her neck and pursed her lips. "Well act like it. Why ain't you at work or something?"

"Because I'm off."

"For how long?" she asked with attitude.

"For as long as you want me to be."

She laughed in his face. "I'm not your patient."

"Anyway, let's change the subject," he paused, "When are you gon' back to school?"

"Oh now, you want to be my daddy too? Well, I don't need him or you tellin' me what to do. I have my grandpa for that and he's the only man I answer to," she said while twisting her neck from side to side.

"Where is he?" he inquired.

"Who?"

"Your father?"

"My father? Oh, he's in heaven."

"I'm sorry."

"Sorry for what?" she asked confused.

"He's dead, isn't he?"

"My father who art in heaven." She giggled. "My earthly 'daddy' I don't know where he is. I ain't never met him."

Amaze at Janiece's response when she told him that her father was in heaven. *A funny sense of humor,* he thought. "Well, I'm sorry about that."

Janiece has never heard of him speak of any earthly father. "Where's yours?"

"He left when I was three," he told her. His face was serious.

"Oh sorry."

"It's cool."

"Do you always act this cool?" she asked.

"What you mean?"

"Do you act this cool when you're in hurtin'?"

"If you had known me a long time ago you would have said I was unpleasant to be around but I thank God and my mama. I had to learn how to forgive so I could be able to move forward."

"Easy for you to say. You haven't had it hard like

me," she answered, her voice growing with aggravation.

"But I couldn't for a long time."

"Really? Doesn't sound like you, Mr. Easy Gon'?"

"I'm not perfect Janiece," he said honestly leaning forward with his hands on his knees.

"Well to me you are. Nothing you can say or do is wrong. Look at how you're tryin' to help me with my messed-up issues."

"That's what friends do."

"Yeah friends," she said quietly, hoping that there was more to it than friendship. Janiece started developing feelings for Josiah after their first 'therapy session'. She felt like she could trust him but she wasn't ready to give her heart to him yet. Then again she didn't know if he wanted her. By no means was she going to tell Jennifer that she had started to develop feelings for Josiah.

Yolanda Adams played over the stereo as she sang in her melodious voice. With her arms still crossed, Janiece leaned back against the sofa and closed her eyes. She started to hum the words first and then sing in her soprano voice.

"Janiece," she heard Josiah call her name after the fifth time. Her eyes popped open as she sat up.

His demeanor was serious. "Wow, you can really sing. I'm impressed," he said as he smiled greatly. He stood up to turn up the song but accidentally switched the song to *Praise Him in Advance* by Marvin Sapp. "Oops, I didn't mean for that to happen but you can really sing," he glared hard into her face and spoke with a humble spirit. "The gift God has given you... is to sing. He wants you to use your singing to glorify him. No offense but you should be singin' in the choir somewhere. Have you been to church lately?"

She shook her head.

"Well, I'd like to take you to church this Sunday."

She stared back. "I can meet you there at eleven a.m."

Sunday morning as promised, Janiece brought along Jennifer as they waited for him. She looked out in the parking lot and saw him. He was dressed in a navy, sleek tailored suit with cognac-colored penny loafers. The corner of her mouth lifted up as she tapped Jennifer on the shoulder. "He's here."

"Good morning," they all greeted each other.

Josiah waved his hand in front of them as they proceeded to enter the church. Jennifer tugged on her arm and whispered in her ear, *"I don't wanna sit in the front now."* Janiece nodded her head. She led them toward the right side of the pews. She glanced throughout the church and spotted her grandparents. They were sitting in their usual spot, upfront. She recalled a memory where she had to suffer upfront with them. Shaking her head at that vision, her feet slid across the burgundy carpet and sat toward the back. As soon as she sat between Jennifer and Josiah, the choir stood up and began to sing, *One of these Days* by her uncle Richard. He produced a soulful tenor. His melodious voice sang, "There'll be no more cryin'. There'll be no more dyin'." While the musical selection comforted her soul, the tears began to fall.

She surrendered to the words of the song as she lifted her hands in the air as she swayed side to side remembering her mama and her daughter. She thanked the Lord silently in her head and then the preacher began the alter call. Many people left their seats and stood in the middle of the congregation. But not Janiece. She sprang to her feet. And stood in place. The music ended and the pastor began citing words.

"We are all standing in the name of the Lord asking for prayer of one's needs or someone else's needs. The Lord says call on me and I will answer you even while you're calling. Now for the ones standing around on this altar, Lord I ask you that you lift each person's burdens and what they may be facing. I don't know what they've gone through or are going through but you know Lord. I ask for breakthroughs, peace, and knowledge to the ones gathered here. It's for our redemption, Lord."

Janiece allowed the tears to flow freely from the corner of her eyes. When the altar call was over, she sat down and wiped her eyes. She felt a calming spirit take over her body to let her know that everything will be all right. She felt Jennifer on her right pat her knee and felt Josiah's hand grab hers. She didn't pull away either because she needed comfort.

The choir began to sing another hit and this was a

song by her Aunt Joann. Her vocal stretched from mezzo-soprano to bass singing. "Don't forget the family prayer...Prayer will teach you right, right from wrong. Prayer will keep your home together; prayer will bring your lost child back home." She realized at that moment that her grandpa hummed that tune the day they dropped off Jennifer.

After church, they walked out to leave. Janiece told Josiah to wait for a few minutes because she had to speak to her grandparents. When she returned to his side, he was standing in the same place. As they began walking to their car, Josiah offered to take them to dinner. She looked over at her friend and her friend made up a lie like she had to do something and suggested she go ahead with Josiah. Janiece eyed her friend before plastering on a fake smile as she walked toward Josiah's '08 black Dodge truck. She watched him pull out his cell phone and speak in a soft tone to his mama.

Chapter 34

Give thanks to the Lord, for he is good!
Psalm 136:1.

Janiece

Shortly after, they pulled up to a one-story brick house with blooming Peonies and Hydrangeas around the front of the house.

"Whose house is this?"

Without looking back, he reached for her hand. "It's my mama's. Don't worry, she's nice."

She got out the truck and her nerves were shot. She felt anxiety was about to take over. She shivered and looked up into his eyes.

"She's cool, don't worry."

She nodded her head and followed him inside his mama's house. He opened the door and walked right in, calling out for his mama. "Umm it sure does smells good in here mama."

His mama wore a cute black dress with an 'Eat my cooking' apron tied around her waist.

"Hey son," she heard his mama's sweet voice.

She examined the interaction between mother and son and it was bittersweet.

"You went to church this mornin'?" Josiah asked his mama as he bent down and kissed her on the cheek.

"I sure did. I went to church with Bessie."

"So did I."

"You did and what brought that on?" she asked bewilderedly, smiling at him.

"A friend," he said smiling, looking back at her.

His mama appeared over his shoulder and looked at her. "Who's this?"

"This is Janiece, mama. Janiece, my mama."

Janiece stuck out her hand but his mama just looked at her hand oddly before engulfing her into a giant hug.

"Good to see you, baby. How you been?"

"Pretty good," was all she said as Josiah told her she could sit at the dining room table.

She pulled out a chair from the table and sat while she observed the interaction between the son and mother. They talked about the small stuff and a slight smile

310

appeared upon her face. He was a *mama's boy*. His mama told them that dinner was ready and asked her what she liked. A plate of cornbread, rice, gravy, Salisbury steak, and broccoli was placed in front of her. Josiah waited for his mama to fix her plate before he began fixing his plate. Soon as they sat at the table to join her, a baritone voice entered the house.

"He ain't never on time to eat," his mama joked while still sitting in her seat.

"Mama," a voice echoed through the house.

Janiece watched as a tall, pecan-complexion guy stepped into the kitchen. He first looked over to her, Josiah, and then his mama. She watched him as he walked over and kissed Josiah's mama on her right cheek. He spoke to Josiah and then his attention turned toward her.

"Janiece this is my younger brother Joshua." Janiece nodded her head as the man came toward her. She stuck out her hand for him to grab it. She waited for his response but he looked down and stared into her eyes.

"Nice to meet you Janiece but we don't shake hands

around here, we hug," he stated as he took her hand and pulled her from her seat and hugged her.

She heard Josiah laugh with a thunderous echo behind her. She hugged the large man back. He was bigger in weight than Josiah. He could pass for a football player.

"You can call me Josh if you like," he winked at her before asking his mama. "What's for dinner?"

"It's some rice, Salisbury steak…"

"I'm sold," he said as he grabbed a plate out of the cabinet.

She watched him pile a lot of food on his plate and joined them in the dining room. He said grace and they had a small conversation as if she was a part of their little family.

"You're a PYT, Janiece. How did you end up with my brotha'?" Joshua asked.

Janiece blinked her eyes a couple of times. *I know he don't think I'm messing with his brother.* She looked over to their mama for interference and thank goodness she told them to take a walk.

"Let's go," was all Josiah stated as they cleared the

plates from the table.

Janiece watched them as they walked out of the house. She picked up the glass of sweet tea and sipped it, looking at their mama eyeing her. *Oh Lord, what is she about to tell me?* Janice thought as she plastered on a coy smile.

"My son is a good man," his mama stated quietly. "He don't mean no harm. He just tried to do what's good."

"I'm sorry, did you say something?" Janiece asked unaware of their pending conversation.

"My oldest son loves his mama."

Janiece said nothing. She didn't know where this conversation was going. She just had to play it by ear.

"He spends too much time workin'."

"That's because he has to. He's soon to be a doctor."

"He bought me this here house when he graduated from medical school. I was so happy." Then her voice changed. She spoke in a soft tone. "It's a long way from the little old shack he grew up in. That house had one bathroom and two bedrooms. It was hard but we

313

managed. When he went to Georgia State, he got a job and every time he would get paid, he would try to send me some money. I told him to save his money until he became a doctor so he could buy his mama a house. It's nice, ain't it?" she asked.

"Yes ma'am, it is."

"His daddy, my ex-husband left us for a younger woman. He had the nerve to tell me that my body ain't like it used to be. I told that man to get outta my face. What, he expected my body to be of a twenty-something year old. I done had two babies. Worked two jobs at one time. I had to keep a roof over our heads and food in our mouth." His mama grinned.

She seemed to amuse herself, Janiece thought. *Dang, she had it bad. But how can she laugh about her husband leaving her having to raise two small boys on her own?*

"When my baby was in the eleventh grade, he got a job and helped around the house and did that until he graduated from college. He did any and everything to help me. Then my youngest son followed behind and got a job. I was so happy when Joshua went off to college. I

314

didn't think he would because he was such a class clown at school. Had me gon' up to that school knowin' I had to work. Hard times bring out the maturity in folks. It seems like you're in a bad situation then it gets worse. But that's all right because the good Lord will see you through. All those hours I had to work, it paid off 'cause my sons are professionals. I ain't got no degree but it's all right 'cause I'm gonna be takin' care of."

"Yes ma'am," was all Janiece said.

"Sugah, there ain't no way but through Jesus."

Not again, she thought. She knew she had some serious talking to do with Jesus when she got home.

"My son needs a good wife. Do you have anybody?" she asked her.

Wife? Hell, I need to find me first before anything else takes residence in my life. Saved by the bell. The Lord must have heard her as she watched Josiah and his brother reenter the house.

"Hey mama, where y'all talkin' about us?" he grinned looking from her to his mama.

Later on Sunday night, Jennifer announced she was

315

going back home. Janiece was depressed but knew she had to go back home. She flipped through the channels on TV. *Diary of a Mad Black Woman* was on BET. She then got up and popped a bag of popcorn in the microwave. Minutes later, she sat back down on the sofa. During the scene Helen (the ex-wife) was dumping her ex-husband in the bathtub filled with water, she started laughing. She thought it was funny.

Then someone started knocking on her door. *Dang, who could this be?* Janiece sauntered toward her apartment door and asked who it was.

"Josiah."

Josiah? What is he doing here? She swung opened the door and gasped. Josiah was standing in front of her, smiling. She figured Jennifer had something to do with Josiah showing up to her apartment unannounced. She was sure to get her later.

"May I come in?" he asked wearing jeans and a blue Polo shirt with white Reeboks.

Janiece looked down and saw that he was carrying a small chocolate cake. She stepped out of the way and allowed him to enter the apartment. Janiece closed and locked the door and led Josiah to the sofa. She watched him as he held onto the cake in his hands tightly and noticed his legs were shaking like he was nervous or something. She was confused as to why he was in her apartment holding cake in his hands but whatever floats his boat. She stepped over him and sat on the sofa.

"Can I put your cake up?" she asked skeptically.

He looked up into her eyes and held a stare. "Yes, I mean no."

"Okay, keep your cake then," she answered annoyed, watching the movie again.

"It's my birthday," his voice was dry.

She giggled. "Well happy birthday to you."

"Thanks, would you like a piece?"

"Yeah," she tossed back. "I have vanilla ice cream." Wanting to know more about why he was here for his birthday instead of celebrating out somewhere she asked herself when she walked into the kitchen, opening the freezer. "If it's your birthday, how come you're here?" she questioned him calmly.

"The best way to share your birthday is to share it with a friend," he smiled.

She wondered how come he didn't mention that earlier but shrugged her shoulder. She offered him a paper plate and a knife to cut the cake. She then took the ice cream out of the freezer. After cutting two slices of cake and spooning ice cream onto their plates, they walked toward the sofa and sat down. Just when Josiah was about to eat a piece of his cake, Janiece stopped him. "What did you wish for?"

He smiled teasingly, "I'm not supposed to say."

"That's right. Happy birthday again."

"Thank you," he said as he bit into his cake and ice cream.

When they finished their dessert, Janiece took his plate to the kitchen and came back and sat on the sofa.

There was silence until he spoke. He then asked her what she did for fun. She chuckled within herself as she thought back over her younger years.

She answered, "I like to go to the movies, skating, bowling, going to nice restaurants, and of course shopping. What about you?"

He chuckled. "I think all women like to go shopping. For myself when I'm off, I like to go fishing, golfing..."

"You look like you would play golf."

"Judgin' me?" he asked playfully, brushing up against her shoulder.

Electricity shot through her and she hoped like hell he felt it too. Janiece played it off. They continued with the small talk and resumed watching the movie in between him asking her questions.

"I...I was wondering," he stuttered.

"What?" she asked playfully, pushing on his shoulder.

"Janiece," he started by name this time. "Would you..."

"What, you shy now all of a sudden?" she asked jokingly. "What you wanna take me somewhere?" she laughed.

"Okay since you wanna clown me," he said jokingly but sternly. "Would you accompany me to the Overton Ball? It's a ball the board put together; a charitable event for doctors and medical students in the fall."

Instead of answering right away, she looked away shyly. He asked her out of all the women he could have taken, wow! *I don't know if I'm truly ready to go out with him like that. I mean I'm attracted to him but going out with him in public, ugh! Should I or should I not? What would Jennifer and Shaneema think? What would her grandparents think? Hell, you might as well have some fun,* she thought.

"You don't have to go if you don't want to," he indicated.

She put her hand up stopping him. "No, I didn't say I wouldn't go. It's just…"

"What?"

She looked away for a moment and then turned back to him. "What're we gon' as?"

"We're gon' as friends."

"Oh, okay. Then I'll go," she stated. "What time and when?"

"It's next Saturday evening at eight. I'll come by and pick you up so we can leave together. Is that okay?" he asked, standing up.

"Yeah, yeah that's fine," she said walking passed him to unlock and open the front door.

She heard him thank her for sharing his birthday with him. When he stepped passed the threshold, Janiece hollered, "Wait!" She ran into the kitchen and grabbed the leftover cake and gave it to him.

"Thanks."

"You're welcome. I'll see you next Saturday."

"See you then," he said as he walked out of the apartment.

The Ending

Chapter 35

My grace is all you need. My power works best in weakness.

2 Corinthians 12:9.

Josiah

When Josiah knocked on Janiece's door, Jennifer opened the door.

"Hello, how're you don'?" she asked.

"I'm good. If I would have known that you would be here, then I would have brought you some flowers as well."

"Aw, that's okay. You sure do look handsome."

"Thank you," he said as he wore a black, multi-stripe suit with a light blue-collar shirt, round button-style cuff links, a blue and white diagonal tie, and black Stacy Adams slip-on shoes.

"Come on in," she said as she opened the door wider.

He was led toward the sofa as he waited for Janiece. As he sat down to engage in conversation with Jennifer, his peripheral view of Janiece made him take a deep breath. His eyes widened with surprise. She was breathtaking. He was taken aback. Her layered bob was in loose curls accentuated with sterling silver drop earrings and a teardrop necklace. The makeup close to natural with a touch of mascara and red lip gloss. She looked stupendous in the black spaghetti strap, chiffon dress. The three-inch stilettos with diamonds across the toes of the shoes did her well. He shoved the flowers at her. After he found his voice, he stated: "Are you ready to go?"

"Yes…yes, I'm ready," she uttered timidly and turned back to a misty-eyed Jennifer. "Can you put these up for me?"

"Sure. Don't do anything that I wouldn't do," she giggled.

Josiah chuckled and shook his head. Josiah was a get to know you type of guy but the way Janiece stood before him made him want to do unjust things to her body. A warm sensation came over him as he glared at her. She was a breathtaking woman standing to the side of him. It wasn't the brother/sister type either. Maybe just maybe God did place him in her life for a reason.

When they arrived at the hotel, they were seated at a

table with eight other guests. Then after the main speech that night, he introduced her to his coworkers as his special friend. They were served chicken cordon bleu, wild rice, green beans, and a roll. They received either sweet tea or lemonade as their drink. After a while, people got up from their seats and strolled toward the dance floor.

He wasn't the type to go on the dance floor unless…As he peered over at Janiece, he could tell she was enjoying her time here the way she was engaging with the other women at the table. He looked down at his watch and when he looked back up he saw a fellow medical student. She was a tall, striking Hispanic woman with curves in the right places. She stopped an inch in front of their table.

"Hey Josiah," she stated as she bent down and kissed him on the cheek.

"Hey Marisol, it's good to see you. Enjoying your night?" he asked looking over to Janiece. She stared at him with raised eyebrows.

Marisol laughed tossing her long hair over her

shoulder and told him yes. She then began to rub on his arm. He thought that was rude. He quickly introduced Marisol to Janiece. Just then a song blared on the speakers.

"Excuse me Marisol, but I'm gon' to ask Janiece to dance," he stated as he watched her smile turn upside down.

He excused himself from her and grabbed Janiece's hand in his.

"May I have this dance?"

She didn't resist him. She placed her hands in his as he led her to the middle of the dance floor with other couples. He listened to Anthony Hamilton's smooth harmonious voice as he sang *Her Heart*. Josiah held her tight but softly in her arms as he rocked her. He thought he heard her sniffle underneath him but wasn't sure. He lifted her chin up and stared at teary stained eyes. He closed his eyes briefly by placing his chin upon her head. They swayed until the song ended. He placed a kiss upon her forehead.

"You ready?" he asked in a deep, sultry tone.

She nodded her head. He grabbed her hands as they walked out of the hotel toward his truck.

"You had a good time?" he asked as she placed the seat belt around her waist.

"I did. How about you?"

"I did. I can't say when the last time was that I enjoyed myself," he said as he turned on the radio. He turned the station to an R&B station that played slow songs. During the ride to her apartment, he felt his heart palpitating and knew his heart won over his mind. He wanted more from Janiece. More like on a permanent basis. He pulled up to her apartment.

"Well, thank you. I had a good time and I'm glad you invited me," she said abruptly, grabbing the door.

Josiah grabbed her arm. "Wait, I have to clear my conscience before I leave you tonight."

"Okay," was all she said.

He couldn't get his words out. He began stuttering. He paused and tried again. "Janiece," he stated softly before turning in her direction. "I've been fightin' this thing I've developed for you for the past month. I tried to tell myself that I'm not supposed to have these kinds of feelings for you but every time I do, you do or say something that changes my way of thinking. It's like you hypnotized me."

"Oh, I'm sorry."

"Shhhh, I meant that in a good way."

"Oh," was her reply.

"What I'm tryin' to say is that I want more of you. I want to take this friendship and turn it into a relationship," he said, "I want you to take me as I am as I have taken you as you are. When I love, I love wholeheartedly. I need you to give me the same if we were to take this to another level. If you don't think you would be able to return the favor then we need to remain as friends. So, are we takin' this to another level or what?"

"You think you can be with someone like me. My past life? I mean how do you know that I'm not suicidal anymore?"

He grabbed her hand in his. "First of all, I know you're not suicidal. You were just gon' through the

328

emotions of what you were gon' through. We all make mistakes. And yes, I want to be with you. What's in the past is in the past. I like the new you or the old you before the streets," his voice held a compassionate tone.

"I don't know. I think I need help findin' myself. Do you really want to take that risk with me? I mean, my past is really messed up."

"Janiece, I'm not like those other guys. I'll be here for you. I don't know but maybe God had something to do with us meetin' that night. It's like a connection. Maybe it's meant to be."

Taking a deep breath and closing her eyes, Janiece opened her mouth. "Yes Josiah, I want to take this chance with you as your girlfriend. I promise to give you my all. As you said before when we love, we love hard. I'm tired of being hurt by men and I promised you if you hurt me in any way, you'll regret it and I'm not playin'."

Josiah chuckled. "You threatenin' me?"

"No. It's more like a promise 'cause I'm tired of being hurt."

"I understand. I plan to go as slow as possible to see

where this relationship takes us."

"Okay," she smiled sweetly. "Can you be a gentleman and walk me to my door?"

"Of course," he said as they both got out the car and walked to her apartment door. Josiah leaned down and gave her a passionate kiss. He waited for Janiece to enter her apartment before driving away in his truck.

Chapter 36

Reprove not a scorner, lest he hate thee: rebuke a wise man, and he will love thee. Proverbs 9:8.

Janiece

For the next few days, while Josiah worked long hours he sent texts throughout the day. She would catch herself smiling at the simplest things he did. He was a *just because* type of guy. On her bad days, she questioned the meaning of his presence in her life. Being with someone like her who's had their heartbroken various times. She shrugged off the negative thoughts as she cleaned the apartment.

Ring. Ring.

She halted her steps and answered the phone. "Hey, you must be on break?"

"Hey to you too baby. But I am to answer your question. What're you plannin' to do this Saturday?"

"Nothin', why, what's up?"

"I was wonderin' if I could take you somewhere."

"Sure. I get off at three," she replied.

"Okay, I'll see you at four."

"Bet."

When Josiah showed up to her place wearing blue jeans, a blue and gray striped shirt, and some black Lugz. She licked her lips.

"Aren't you cute? Who are you lookin' cute for?" Janiece joked.

"You," he said as he planted kisses all over her face.

She looked over her attire and hoped it was appropriate for wherever he was taking her. She sported blue jeans, a purple baby-doll camisole with low heel boots. As Josiah drove, he reached over with his right hand and grabbed her left hand and held it. He soon pulled up at LaGrange's Museum. She always wanted to visit here but thought she would get looked down upon. Her heart swelled with glee. When they got the truck, he walked around and grabbed her hand as they entered the museum. After the museum, Josiah told her he was taking her to one of her favorite spots. When he pulled to the mall and parked in front of JCPenney, her heart sped up. She felt her heart palpitate. Was she freaking out? Oh shit! What if she saw them? She was very quiet. She felt Josiah turned toward her rather than saw him.

"I know that dress cost you an arm and a leg. I just want to repay you back."

"That's fine. You don't have to repay me. Remember we're in a relationship so you don't have to do that."

"Well," he stated. "Why don't we go in and if you see anything you want, tell me and it's yours."

"Really, you don't have to."

He frowned. "What happened to you tellin' me that you love shoppin'?"

"I do but we don't have to do it today."

"Janiece, you know that I'm not gon' to let up, right?"

"Yeah, but I was hopin' tho," she laughed out loud as she opened the door and stretched, waiting for him to come around to her side.

When they walked inside JCPenney, Janiece saw a clearance sign on bras and panties. "You're not scared to come in the lingerie department, are you?"

He chuckled as he followed her toward the lingerie department. She picked up two bras, a pair of barely-there stockings, and four panties. Josiah paid for the items because he was treating her today. They strolled outside of JCPenney and into the mall. Next stop Radio Shack because Josiah wanted to check out the GPS systems. Walking out of Radio Shack, she spotted Mya. She turned her head. Put her hand over her face.

"Janiece! Janiece!" Mya yelled from across the hall.

"Somebody is callin' for you," Josiah told her as they walked passed Payless Shoe Store.

Janiece waved her hands in the air and said, "It ain't nobody."

"Oh," was all he said.

When she stood on the outside of Bath and Bodyworks, smelling some of the candles they had on display. She picked up the 'Mahogany Teakwood' candle. It smelled like a man. Without it being lit, it had a powerful scent. Seconds later, she felt a tap on her shoulder. Her heart paused briefly.

"Hey girl, where you been?"

"Around," Janiece spoke in a nonchalant manner, not even turning around to face Mya.

"Damn girl, you look good too."

This time she turned around and glared at the annoying friend she used to have. "Thanks but we have to get gon'," her eyes fixed on her boyfriend. Oblivious to her emotional mood, he held her JCPenney bag.

"Girl, who is this fine muthafucka here?"

Janiece's eyes grew wide. She moved in front of Josiah. "This is my boyfriend," she said in a proud tone.

"Girl, I can see why you got with him. He's packin'," Mya said, glancing at his crotch. "Girl, you ain't gonna introduce me?" Mya asked with an attitude. "Since you so rude, I'm Mya."

Janiece watched Josiah take Mya's hand and shake it. He turned to look at her for further introduction.

"I'm a friend of yo' girl here. We go way back, don't we girl? What happened that day you left my crib?"

"Ex-friend."

"Ex?" Mya questioned angrily. "Oh, so you all siddity now since you got a man that's paid. He must be hittin' it right too."

She could tell by Josiah's face that he was shocked at

her words but not her.

"Girl don't act like you ain't had no dick before. Anyway, Ritz and my man should be here anytime soon," she said, "Oh, here they are."

The blood rushed to her brain. A slight throb thumped on the left side of her head. Sweat appeared upon her forehead as the scene unfolded before her eyes. This could not be happening. Janiece quickly peeked at Josiah. He stood calmly beside her. She didn't want to introduce any of this in his life. He deserved more. She deserved more. As Ritz and Derrell stopped in front of them, Josiah closed the gap and now stood in front of her.

She was happy to see that her boyfriend stood up to have her back.

"Sup man, what seems to be the problem?" Josiah asked with a smug look across his face.

"Oh shit, she done got a bodyguard," Derrell joked.

"I would hope so afta that trick you pulled," Ritz spat out. He was referring to his rival Trane.

"I know right," Mya agreed as she smacked her lips.

Janiece just stared at them. She felt Josiah grab her

hand and pulled her away. "It's time for us to go. And don't worry about her well-being. Know that she has a good man that will protect her."

"Where were you that night when she..." Derrell was interrupted by her remark.

She snatched her hand out of Josiah's and snapped. "Shut the fuck up, you bastards! All of y'all are gon' straight to hell!" she said as they marched to the entrance of JCPenney.

They walked so fast in and out of JCPenney. They were beside his truck within minutes. She said nothing as Josiah unlocked the truck. She slid in and was thankful he didn't try talking to her. She needed to forget it ever happened. They made it back to her apartment in record time. She opened her door and laid down on the sofa.

"Drink some water," he said handing her the glass.

Janiece didn't budge. She lay balled up in a fetal position on the sofa with a pillow covering her face. She hoped he got the message. To leave her alone. But unfortunately, she felt a dip in the sofa and knew he was sitting next to her.

"You wanna talk about it?"

"No."

"I'm not gon' to let up. I'm here if you need me," he whispered, rubbing her across the shoulder with his strong hand.

Janiece pushed the pillow away and sat up quickly. With tear-stained eyes, she yelled, "Well, maybe I don't need you. I have too much baggage that you can't handle!"

In his comforting voice, "I'm not gon' anywhere so get over it. I don't want you to do something…"

"Before I what! Try to kill myself again, huh? Is that what you were gon' to say? Say it."

"No, I was gon' to say do something crazy."

"What's the difference between crazy and suicidal? I can't take this shit. Get out! You're just like them. You're gonna turn on me too. I want to be by myself for a while," she cried.

"Okay, I'll leave you alone for the rest of the night," he stood up.

"No!" she screamed. "I don't want you to ever come

338

back."

"Look here Janiece," he declared as he spun around to her. "I don't know what your problem is but I'm not like them. Don't ever compare me to those lowlifes. If you want it your way, then fine I'm gone. You don't have to worry about me ever comin' to your rescue because I am finished tryin' to help you. Something is literally wrong with you. You need to suck it up and get over it," he roared as he walked toward the front door.

She heard his footsteps walking toward the door. She sprang to her feet, lunged toward him and yelled, "Don't go!"

He turned slowly, "What?"

Hanging on to his sleeve, she whimpered as she wiped her eyes. "I'm sorry. Don't leave me. I can't take anyone else leavin' me right now. I'm sorry. I'm just angry with them for lying on me. What they said about me ain't true. Don't leave me, Josiah," she cried uncontrollably while he locked his arms around her.

"I'm sorry too," he apologized.

"Why do you care so much? Why do you want me? I

don't know how to love," she sobbed in his arms.

"Because I see something in you that you don't see in yourself," he confessed, holding her tightly.

"What do you see?" she asked glaring at his concerned face.

"I see a warrior. I see a person who is fighting to be strong for everyone but herself. I see a survivor. Who's survived so much already," he stated as he held onto her as her anger subsided.

Chapter 37

For you, I'd share the cup of love that overflows...I'd change all thoughts I have of you. Kenny Lattimore.

Janiece

A few minutes later, Janiece talked to Josiah about her feelings about what had transpired at the mall. "I'm really sorry Josiah. I do want this to work."

"I know you do and so do I. Let's put this behind us and talk about something else," he said as he wiped a lonely tear away as he kissed her forehead.

She giggled. "What would that be?"

"When am I gon' to meet your grandparents?"

"Good question. Um, how about Thanksgiving?"

"Sounds good to me."

"What about your mama? I don't wanna leave her out."

He pulled back a strand of hair out of her face. "Look at my girl, caring about my mama for Thanksgiving. She'll be okay."

She laid in between his legs as he rubbed her arms up

and down. "How about I invite both of you? You think she'll come?"

"I'll have to ask."

"Okay, so Mr. Tate tell me something about you that I don't know."

"Like what?" he asked dumbfounded.

"Like anything."

"I'm almost finished interning and hopefully I'll be a cardiologist in one year."

"No duh!"

"I like children and would love someday to have some on my own."

"Okay. Well since you're being so secretive and all. Ima asks you some questions," she shifted beside him. "Since we're in a relationship, right? I can ask you anything, right?"

"Sure," he said.

"How good of a man are you?" she asked with arched eyebrows.

He chuckled. "I'm a virgin, partially."

"Oh my gosh, are you serious?" she asked jokingly

then turned serious. "What you mean partially?"

"I mean I haven't had intercourse yet."

"You alright down there?" she asked pointing to his crotch.

"So far as I know of, yeah."

"How come you've never lost your virginity?"

"Funny, huh?" he asked.

"Kinda. I mean, I ain't never heard of no twenty-nine-year-old who's still a virgin. It's kinda cool actually. I just wished I could have stayed one as long as you have done."

"Yeah, it's not that appealing if you know what I mean. I was focused on graduating and providing for my mama instead of worrying about a woman," he stated.

"Why you say partially a virgin?"

"Back in college, a classmate of mine was supposed to help me study but ended up helping herself when she gave me head."

"Why you say helpin' herself instead of you?" she asked inquisitively.

"Because that is what she did. I didn't ask for that."

She chuckled. "Then you're still a virgin."

"Not by a long shot," he laughed. "Janiece?" he asked in a serious tone.

"Yeah."

"Do you plan to go back to school?"

"I do when I save enough money from work. Why? Does it bother you that I'm not gon' to school right now?"

"No Janiece," he sighed. "I just asked."

"Well if its gon' to be a problem for you let me know and I'll bounce. Don't want to be nobody's charity case."

"Janiece," he grabbed her face with his hands and pulled her face close to his. "Why won't you let somebody love you just the way you are?"

"I'm sorry," was all she said with her head bowed.

"Stop apologizin'," he stated. "If you don't like your life, then do something."

"I hear you, daddy," she said in a seductive tone.

"I'm not your daddy so don't call me that."

"I'm sorry."

"All is forgiven. Now let me kiss you."

344

Thanksgiving day, only Josiah showed up at Janiece's door. "Where's your mama?"

"She told me to tell you Happy Thanksgiving and make sure I eat enough to carry me when I go back to work tomorrow."

"Yes, ma'am," she said as she followed Josiah out to his truck. She gave him directions to her grandparents' house.

Knock. Knock.

Her grandpa answered the door in blue overalls and a striped shirt.

"Hey baby girl," he grabbed, hugged and kissed her on the forehead. Then he looked to the side of her at her guest.

"Grandpa, I would like for you to meet my boyfriend Josiah," her grandpa eyed her suspiciously. "He's a good guy like you, Grandpa."

"I'll have to see for myself," he said as he reached out his hand toward Josiah.

Josiah shook his hand. "Hello, Mr. Willie. I'm soon to

be Dr. Josiah Tate."

Janiece looked up at Josiah and wondered why he introduced himself like that.

"Being a doctor don't mean anything. Takin' good care of my baby girl is what I'm lookin' for. But it's good to meet you, Josiah."

"You too sir."

While they entered the house, Janiece leaned over and nudged Josiah on the elbow. "That doctor stuff doesn't work with my grandpa. Havin' a title behind your name doesn't mean much. It's the person's character that he looks for. You have to be yourself and leave out the doctor part from now on."

Sooner than later she knew her grandpa was going to joke with her grandma about Josiah.

"Honey, this here is a doctor," her grandpa said in his southern voice.

"Uh, I've met a lot of doctors in my lifetime and they can't tell me nothin'."

Janiece chuckled and nudged Josiah in the ribs. He set himself up to be picked on. After introductions the right way, they were all seated at the kitchen table. Her grandpa said grace and they dug in. They ate and had a pleasant conversation at dinner. At the dinner table, Grandma and Grandpa both told embarrassing stories about her.

For Christmas, they spent time apart. Josiah worked Christmas day. He was going to spend the rest with his family. Janiece spent time with her grandparents and then Jennifer afterward. She got a text from Josiah later on that night that she would spend New Year's Eve with him.

Chapter 38

"My wayward children", says the Lord, "come back to me, and I will heal your wayward hearts." Jeremiah 3:22.

Janiece

Josiah and Janiece attended church together after New Year's Day. Janiece wore a peach blouse with a peachy, flowery skirt with brown boots. Josiah sported black slacks, a striped, long sleeve shirt, and black Loafers as they sat side by side in the middle of the congregation. The service went smoothly for Janiece until now. When the choir began singing, it hit a nerve. Tears began to trickle down her cheeks.

"God has smiled on me; he has set me free. God has smiled on me, he been good to me," the choir sang the chorus twice before singing a verse of the completed song. "Amazing sight, the Savior stands and knocks at every door. Ten thousand blessings in his hands to satisfy the soul. Ain't you glad," the piano player said to the choir. The choir singing the chorus part again before ending the song.

Janiece stood up and swayed side to side when the choir sang as the tears flowed. Her mind and spirit were into the song. She was focused on the song and no one else. When the choir finished singing, there was tons of clapping and praising for the song.

When the preacher walked to the podium, he said gleefully, "All sinners are welcomed to the House of the Lord. Let the church say amen."

"Amen," the congregation said in unison.

"Now let us turn to the book of Numbers chapter twenty-one verses four through nine," she heard the pastor say. "God allows tragedy to shake us out of our selfishness."

Yep, this sermon was meant for her again. She listened intently as the pastor preached. He continued, "He allows things to happen to us to get us to focus on him. When a loved one dies, when we lose our jobs, we-uh-we are forced out of our living quarters and have to stay with a relative to get back on our feet. He allows those things to happen. To wake us up and know that he is in charge."

"In Numbers twenty-one, four through nine, God had directed the Israelites to the long way out of Mount Hor, to avoid the Edomites. However, uh-uh the Israelites became impatient. So uh they began to complain to God and Moses. So they turned from God and did their own thing. God did not bless them with a miracle, instead He sent snakes in the village causing death to many of them. That's when they turned back and confessed their sins to Moses to ask God for interference."

He continued, "When tragedy strikes us, it's a personal way in which God communicates with His people. We may not know what God has planned for us but we need to look for His divine purpose and instruction."

Halfway during the sermon, Janiece believed her knowledge of understanding God increased more and more spiritually. She felt her burdens being lifted as he spoke the Word. Yes, she was learning how to forgive and move forward.

"Now let the church say amen."

"Amen," they said.

"As we close today-Is there anyone who lost a loved one, ain't got no job no more or no home to go to, someone is strung out on drugs or havin' problems with their children please come. As Jesus said, 'finding the lost sheep is better than havin' the ninety-nine sheep who were already saved.' If there's anyone, please let him come. Just remember God loves and cares so much that once you're in His power, you won't need to seek anything but the love of Jesus. Yes, Jesus died for our sins that we may be able to live. If Jesus is worthy of our love, don't you think you're worthy to give yourself to him? In Jesus' name, amen."

Janiece let go of Josiah's hand and stood up. She passed by a couple of people who were sitting in the pew before proceeding her way down the aisle of the church with tears drenching her face. She stood with outstretched hands to the heavens and cried out, thanking the Lord.

She whispered, "Forgive me, Father."

After church, she was greeted by her grandparents as Josiah stood by her side. They were thankful that Janiece was back on track for good. Later, they had dinner at her grandparents' house.

Later that night in her apartment, Janiece knew that it was time. It had been a long time since she prayed for herself. She knelt down on her knees, put her hands together, and bowed her head on the edge of her bed.

"Our Father who art in heaven, Father I come to you with a repentant heart. I've been in the dark too long. I've been bitter. Hateful. Lost. Weak. Depressed. I'm tired of crying day and night. I want to be released from this emotional bondage. I'm tired of not belonging to you. I want my prayer heard. Hear me, Lord. Forgive my afflictions of wandering and things unspoken of for I rebelled against your ways. Father, I know I was wrong to doubt you loved my child and little ol' me," she pointed her index finger at her chest. "I know Father that you are sincere in forgiving us for our sins. Father, I'm truly sorry," her palms were facing upward, "for letting myself go after my baby died but I now know that you'll put nothing more on us than we can bare. I know my sins tore us apart. I went left and you told me to go right. You state you'll wash away my sins if I trust and believe in you. I ask that you hear my cry. Cover me. I'm kneeling in need of prayer and comfort."

"Only you can make me whole again. God, you're many names. You're a healer, deliverer, you're the author and the finisher. I thank you, Father, for wakin' me up and renewin' my spirit in your love. I have hope in things unseen because I believe in you. For your mercies endureth forever. I know you can turn my pain into something glorious. I pray that you set me apart again. I'm your willing servant," she sobbed. "I just know that you have a better plan for me, Father. I continue to ask you to strengthen me where I'm weak Lord. I'm weak Lord. This soldier of yours is weak but with faith, I can be made strong again," she shouted through fresh and dried tears. "Thank you, Jesus. I give you praise. In Jesus' name, I pray. Amen," she said as she stood up and scooted herself in bed. She knew great things were to follow her. As she wrapped herself under the covers, the rustling of papers on her nightstand stopped her in her tracks, she focused on the papers and associated that to

God answering her prayer.

Chapter 39

Love is a temple. Love is a higher love. Mary J. Blige & U2.

Josiah

He had stopped by his mama's house like every Saturday morning when he was off. He had to tell someone and that someone wasn't his brother at the moment. It was his mama. Last night he couldn't sleep well even working late due to tossing and turning. He had a lot on his mind. Josiah's heart and mind were clashing with each other constantly for the past weeks. His mind was telling him that she has problems and to stay away but his heart was letting him know that she needed him in this journey. He cared for Janiece and knew he could grow to love her fervently in the Lord. He wanted her to share his love of faith as his wife and believed she was on her path to healing for herself because she overcame so much in the past. He knew the person she was now and what was behind her was behind her. He wanted to be there through thick and thin with her healing process. He wanted a woman after his own heart after chasing God first. He wanted to be that man beside her and it caused his heart to swell with a strong passion for endurance. He *was* in love with the Janiece he saw.

At the beginning of their relationship, he knew they couldn't remain as friends because he felt a strong connection. It wasn't because of her looks only. He wasn't that type to get with a young woman just because of her looks. It was her struggle, her endurance, her survival, and the healing was what attracted her to him. She had been through the worst losing two people in her life at a young age. He couldn't imagine but she survived. He just hoped Janiece was ready for what he was planning to propose to her. They could take as long as she wanted or as soon. He wanted Janiece as his wife. And he knew that his mama wanted grandchildren so why couldn't he have the best of both worlds? Love conquered all in his book.

"Mama, I think she is the one," he announced to his mama as he held a cup of toasted almond coffee in his right hand.

He stared at the backside of his mama as she was scrambling the eggs. He watched her as she turned the pot of grits on low and checked the bacon in the oven. He waited for a reply from his mama.

"You think or you know?" he heard her speak without turning around.

"I know and mama I can't be any happier that I found what I was lookin' for in Janiece. I found someone whom I trust in everything. She's everything I ever wanted in a wife. She's a survivor, humble, goofy, sarcastic, and beautiful on the inside and the outside. I know she's been through a lot and I'm willing to stand behind and beside her to help her onto recovery. She's getting to relearn how God works. We both believe in God the Father and Jesus as the only begotten Son and the Holy Spirit who convicts us. She's a born-again servant and knows that Christ is her true Savior."

"That's good son. I'm happy for you but I don't want you to rush into anything to please me or set yourself up."

"Set myself up?" he asked, placing his coffee cup down on the table.

"Makin' her your wife to get her in your bed. I know that's the only way you'll have sex with a woman if you married her." His mama turned around facing him with her cooked meal in her hands.

Josiah smiled at his mama's comment. He *loved* her. No sex would amount to the way he felt about her. "No mama, it's not that at all. Can I have your blessing?"

"Of course, you—" he watched her as she placed her food on the table before coming to stand in front of him. She bent down and kissed him on his forehead. "You have to work at marriage. It's no easy task. She's coming from a troubled background. When you marry, you marry for a lifetime. Not one of these celebrity marriages to get a divorce in a month. In First Peter three, seven, it says, 'You husbands must give honor to your wives. Treat your wife with understanding as you live together. She may be weaker than you are, but she is your equal partner in God's gift of new life. Treat her as you should so your prayers will not be hindered.'"

"I understand ma and happy to know that you're with me."

"I love you."

"I love you too," was al he said.

"Now go make that woman happy by askin' her hand in marriage."

"Yes ma'am," he said as he rose from the kitchen table. He placed his empty cup in the sink.

He started walking toward the front door when he heard his mama call his name as he placed his right hand on the doorknob.

"What if she says no?"

"I'll have to deal with that as well," he said and turned back toward the front door.

Josiah sent Janiece a text and asked if she could meet him at the Calloway Garden as he drove over there himself. When he pulled into the parking lot, she wasn't there yet. *Thank God*, he thought. He pulled out the ring he bought a couple of weeks ago from the glove compartment. As he fingered the ring, his mind started to ramble again. Was he moving too fast? What if her past comes back? What if she? Just then he saw her car pull next to him and shuffled the ring inside of his coat pocket. He got out and watched her step out of her car wearing jeans, long sleeve shirt with a long black cardigan. The breezy weather was cool but not cold on this day.

"Hey Josiah," she greeted him with warmth as she pecked a kiss upon his lips.

He looked down into her onyx expressive, brown eyes accentuated with her fawn complexion. In the winter, her light-yellow brown skin turned paler.

They embraced each other and started walking through the garden. They walked one mile in the garden when Josiah spotted a bench.

"Let's take a break," he announced.

Janiece joked. "I thought you were in shape. I know you ain't tired already."

"I know right," he said, stretching before pulling her down on the bench beside him. He opened his mouth but saw a Caucasian couple. He waited till they passed before he faced Janiece. He looked over her while she was admiring the bushes of reds, yellow, pink, and white roses. *Do it now*, he thought.

"Stand upright quick," he uttered.

Janiece jumped up quickly and started brushing her cardigan off. "Was it a bug?"

He cracked a smile. "Nah," he answered as he reached inside his jacket and pulled out a small box.

"Hey, I thought we were gonna eat at a restaurant to exchange our gifts. You cheated 'cause mine is in the car and if I go all the way back to the car you can bet I ain't comin' back this way. I want to enjoy the garden for a while."

"You can. I just want to give this to you now," he said in a serious tone, giving her the box.

"What is it?" she asked as she took the box from his hand and opened it. Her eyes widened in disbelief. Her thoughts were scattered. "Are you serious? Is this what I think this is?"

His grin deepened as he glared at her.

She took a step back and her mouth dropped to the 'O' shape. "Are you serious?"

"Yes," he stated as he dropped down to one knee. "Janiece, I cared deeply for you when I first saw you," he stated as he grabbed her left hand.

"That was—" she was cut off by him.

"I fell in love with you at the ball and I know that sounds corny but it's true. I know we will have to work at this thing called love."

Her right hand covered her mouth instantly as the tears welled up in her eyes. She blinked her eyes but they fell.

"Janiece, will you do me the honor of becoming my wife?"

Glancing up at her, the tears continue to fall. "I'm willing to wait for us. We can have a long engagement or as short as you want. But I want you. I know you have a past. I have a past too. I'm willing to work on us to see where life takes us on this journey. I wouldn't want to do it with anyone else but with you."

There he said it. He waited. And waited.

"Janiece," he whispered as his voice cracked.

Her eyes blinked several times before she spoke to him. For a moment, he was scared.

"You're askin' me?" she pointed her index finger at

her chest.

He nodded his head.

"A troubled soul like me?" she asked with hesitation. "You asked me to be a future doctor's wife?"

"Yes," he answered cautiously.

"Yes!"

Thank God, she finally answered yes, he thought as he shoved the ring onto her left ring finger. He jumped for joy as he spun her around and planted kisses all over her face.

When he placed Janiece back on her feet, he reassured her that nothing sexually changed between them. He wanted to wait until their wedding night and she agreed. After agreeing to become his wife, she leaned into his arm as they walked back to their car that she wanted to tell her grandparents right away.

He followed her to her grandparents' house. She led the way and he trailed behind her inside the house. Janiece was quick to flash her left hand. He watched her grandparents' stoic faces. He could tell they were surprised. With a lot of convincing, her grandparent's slowly accepted the ordeal. His heart swelled to see Janiece's eyes light up as she was surrounded by her family.

"You know marriage is hard Janiece. And when you feel like givin' up don't because there ain't nothin' like havin' your own husband. Y'all will have to learn to compromise on a lot of things in your marriage. Don't let others in, especially other women who ain't family. Keep your sex life to yourself," her grandma announced shockingly.

"Grandma!" Janiece hollered.

"Listen to your grandma," her grandpa said as he kept his eyes on him.

Josiah wasn't intimidated by her grandpa. He felt he was trying to do the right thing and make sure he wasn't all talk.

"I'm tellin' you what I know. You don't want them up in yo business. They will go behind your back and try to sneak in on your husband. Remember that."

"Yes ma'am," was all Janiece stated.

"So when is the big day?" her grandma asked

cheesing like a Cheshire cat.

"I don't know. We haven't discussed it," she turned to stare at Josiah. "Josiah, I must say that I'm really happy that you were the one who saved me that day. You came into my life when there was no one to turn to," she paused, "I say thank you in front of my grandparents to let them know that I'm truly grateful for you and that we're meant to be together. It seems as if you've erased my past."

Before he could respond, her grandpa answered. "Honey, when two people are put together and want to work together. They have to leave it all behind if they expect a future together."

"That's right, Mr. Willie. I agree with you."

"Do you love our Janiece wholeheartedly?" her grandpa questioned.

"I do and like I told her earlier, I'm willing to help her emotionally, mentally, and spiritually to overcome."

"That's so beautiful," her grandma stated as she started tearing up.

"Remember to put God first."

Her grandpa told them to grab hands as he prepared to pray over their union. When they said amen, her grandpa ordered him to step outside for a few minutes with his hand. Janiece shook her head at her grandpa. She knew he was giving Josiah, 'the talk.' Fifteen months later, Josiah and Janiece were married at the church.

Chapter 40

My lover is to me a sachet of myrrh resting between my breasts. Songs of Solomon 1:13.

Janiece

When they tied the knots fifteen months ago, her lease on the apartment ran its course and then she moved in with Josiah. As she lay in her pink, lace negligee waiting on her husband to come out of the bathroom. She couldn't believe she was a married woman. Who knew her life would turn out like this? She thanked God in her head. She had moved on from her past and knew she had more mountains to climb and knew she could get through them by holding onto her faith.

When the bathroom door opened, she watched as her sexy man strolled to her wearing pink boxers just for her. Janiece giggled and squirmed onto the silken sheets underneath her as she watched his taunt abs glistening of caramelized skin. Her smile widened as he did a silly dance, gyrating his hips as he stood in front of her. He eased his way onto the bed, crawling and then hovering over her. In a heated passion, he bent down and kissed her on the lips.

He breathed, "You ready?"

She nodded her head as she gazed into his dark eyes. His natural manly scent enticed her immensely. She never had a man to take his time with her as much as Josiah did.

He then rubbed his right hand across her hip up to her breast. Next, he squeezed her breast before devouring her breast through the negligee. He kissed them softly and then began unbuttoning the negligee. He circled his tongue around her nipple.

She squealed underneath his touch as unpleasant memories were resurfacing to the top of her mind.

"You okay?"

She gawked at a frightened Josiah and nodded her head.

He kissed his way down toward her belly button, licking around her navel and skipping over her core. He went straight to her toes.

This time she squirmed and pulled him back up toward her. He kissed her on the lips and then began massaging her right leg. She was so wet with her moistness that she was ready for Josiah, she thought. She closed her eyes as she moved upward toward the headboard and he followed with a questioning look in his eyes.

She smiled playfully. She summoned him with her finger and winked at him. Josiah suckled her breast like a newborn baby. Made his way from her breast to her chest, belly, neck, and then her ears.

Oh shit! This is the spot, she mused as she closed her eyes as he nestled into her hidden aphrodisiac spot.

She moaned in pleasure, "Ahhhhh."

She felt Josiah leave her spot. He moved down her stomach by kissing all over until he came to her navel. He sucked her navel and she giggled. He then moved closer to her core, rubbed his nose over her thong and stopped. All of a sudden, he started tickling her. She tried to get him to stop tickling her but it was no use to his power. So she laughed as he tickled her.

"Okay, I'll stop," he said seductively. "I want to take this real slow. I want to make love to my wife.

Wife, she mused as Josiah lay on top of her. He used his knees to open up her legs as she laid waiting on her husband. He started once again kissing her lips. And then the kissing increased. Slow and gentle turned into hot and passionate French kissing. He moved down toward her panties. She lifted her hips as he gently pulled the panties off.

He glanced up and whispered to her, "We're born again virgins—"

She burst into a waterfall of tears.

"I know baby." His voice dripping in silk. It was rich.

"It's gon' to be okay. It's a new beginnin' for us as husband and wife," he kissed her on the lips as the tears wouldn't stop falling.

She blinked her eyes repeatedly as he hovered over her, wide-eyed. He held himself up on his left elbow as he slipped off his boxers. He spread her legs wider with his right knee. Held his manhood in his hands while he repositioned himself in between her legs.

"I was raped," she announced with disgust as she laid underneath his deep gaze.

"What!" he hollered.

"I was raped on my eighteenth birthday," she whispered.

"Shit baby! We don't have to do this now. We can wait until tomorrow," he said with a sorrowful tone as he held her in his arms. I'm so sorry," he planted kisses over her face.

As the tears ran down the side of her face, she cried. "It's okay. It's our wedding night."

"I know and tomorrow it will be even better."

"Josiah, I'm sorry."

"It's okay. I'll wait Mrs. Tate."

"Thank you," she said as she hugged him back. She hated to dish that part of her life to him now but felt he needed to know everything about her. Certain positions reminded her of that terrible time. She cried until the tears wouldn't fall any longer. They lay in bed cuddling until they both fell asleep hours later.

The next night, Janiece was ready for her husband to make love to her. She wore nothing as he slipped under the covers. He beamed as he kissed her lips and touched all over her body before mounting her. Janiece felt safe and secure with him since he knew the truth. During their lovemaking, Josiah panted and sweated. Just when he was about to come, he gazed into her loving eyes and mouthed, *I love you* as his seeds emptied into her core.

Acknowledgments

First, I would like to thank the Holy Trinity. Without them, I would be lost. I thank God for giving me this gift of writing. To be able to come up with stories at the top of my head that might inspire someone someday. I remember a long time ago, I thought I didn't have a gift. I read about the gifts of prophesying, preaching, singing, and others. In remembrance of my mother, she stated, 'I stepped out of line too early for singing because I come from a musical background', LOL! Secondly, I'd like to thank my true supporters such as my children, sister Jaime, brother Kelvin, and cousins. Thanks to my home church Newness of Life Baptist for the beautiful songs provided in this story and in remembrance of Uncle Richard, 'the steps of a good man'. Thank you for taking this heartfelt journey with Janiece and Josiah. And a big thanks to all the upcoming readers, reviewers, and fans!! Thanks for the feedback, love, and support.

I believe!!!

With Love,

Sigourney Moore

You can find me on Facebook: S. Cassadera

www.facebook.com/Sigourney.moore79

You can email me: S.cassadera@aol.com

amazon.com/author/scassadera

Book Club Questions

1. Have you ever came close to a decision like Janiece when she hit rock bottom?

2. Does God really forgive us?

3. Are you a lukewarm person when it comes to having a relationship with God when tragedy strikes against you?

4. Have you established an intimate relationship with God?

5. Although brought up in church, is it possible for a person to stray away from the Word when we experience a loss?

6. Is it appropriate for a white person 'who's down' to say the word 'nigga'?

7. What's your 'go-to' inspirational song that helps bring you out of your despair/depression?

8. Is there another way to be saved spiritually?

9. If you don't believe in God, do you believe in some spiritual being(s)?

10. Have you ever experience a loss? Did it draw you closer or push you away from God?

11. Does God look at the heart or the sins of a person?

12. Do you believe in the Bible in its entirety?

13. Do you believe you'll be able to see your loved ones in heaven one day?

14. Why is it taboo for black people to see a therapist?

To submit a manuscript to be considered, email us at submissions@majorkeypublishing.com

Be sure to <u>LIKE</u> our Major Key

Publishing page on Facebook!

CPSIA information can be obtained
at www.ICGtesting.com
Printed in the USA
LVHW041727011020
667692LV00003B/680